QUESTS & SPELLS

Fairy tales from the European oral tradition

edited and annotated by

Judy Sierra

BOB KAMINSKI MEDIA ARTS

Bob Kaminski Media Arts
183 Garfield Street
Ashland, Oregon 97520
(503) 482-1328

Library of Congress Cataloging-in-Publication Data:

Quests & spells : fairy tales from the European oral tradition / edited and annotated by Judy Sierra.
    p.   cm.
  Includes bibliographical references.
  Summary: Presents eighteen tales collected from European storytellers of the nineteenth century.
  ISBN 0-9636089-2-4 : $12.95
  1. Fairy tales--Europe. 2. Tales--Europe. [1. Fairy tales. 2. Folklore--Europe.] I. Sierra, Judy. II Title: Quests and spells.
PZ8.Q36   1994
398.2'09401--dc20   94-22003
                                       CIP

Contents

What is a fairy tale?

Although many kinds of fantasy stories are called fairy tales nowadays, the tales in this book are drawn from a European storytelling tradition that dates back thousands of years. The oral fairy tales of Europe are a group of closely intertwined stories that have similar characters, episodes, and magical elements. The European fairy tale tradition transcends the boundaries of language and nation.

Most fairy tales are success stories in which a young hero or heroine's goodness is recognized and rewarded. Worthy young people acquire magical objects, powers, or helpers as they set out to prove themselves in the adult world. Fairy tales may be related to the initiation rituals of earlier times. The world of the fairy tale is not that of everyday life, but it is not a place where just anything can happen. It is a realm where magic works in very predictable ways. Humans are transformed into animals and vice-versa. Evil spells are cast, then broken, and the person responsible for such evil is suitably punished. The successful fairy tale quest is nearly always followed by a marriage, though many oral fairy tales continue beyond the wedding.

Children love the magic and adventure in fairy tales. They identify with the heroes and heroines who, though they are neglected or mistreated, and may be small and weak, always triumph in the end. Fairy tales offer the promise of happiness in even the most hopeless of cases.

Adults read fairy tales for enjoyment, and also as a way of seeing patterns of meaning in their lives. Fairy tales from the oral tradition offer us a rich resource of symbols and metaphors for psychological interpretation. Though they may not depict the best of all possible worlds, they can help us understand the world we have been given.

I have not included any tales of Hans Christian Andersen, Charles Perrault, or Jacob and Wilhelm Grimm in this collection. Perrault and Andersen were literary artists who were inspired by oral fairy tales. The Grimms' tales are much closer to oral tradition, but I have chosen not to include them since they are so widely available. Many of the tales that follow are similar to the Grimms' tales, yet they are richer in detail and more faithful to the coherent belief system upon which the fairy tales are based. They can help clarify some of the puzzling aspects of better-known fairy tales. After a reading of "Prince Lindorm," the enchantment and disenchantment of the Frog Prince no longer seem quite so strange or inexplicable. The tale of "Twelve Wild Ducks" suggests the possibility that the seven dwarves had met Snow White before.

In notes at the end of this book, I explore the relationships among tales, as well as some of the fascinating connections between fairy tales and European legends, myths, rituals and folk belief.

The Three Princes, the Three Dragons, and the Old Woman with the Iron Nose

[HUNGARY]

y the shores of the Blue Sea, there was a land where dragons grew, and this land was ruled by a king whose court was draped in black and whose eyes never ceased to weep, for every Friday he had to send nine and ninety young men to be devoured by a pack of dragons. This king had three sons, each more handsome and more clever than the other. The eldest was named Andrew, the middle son was Emerich, and the youngest was Ambrose. Finally the Friday arrived when the king's three sons were the only young men left alive in the land. Andrew and Emerich went to their father and begged him to allow them to go and fight the dragons. They were certain they could defeat them and end the suffering in their kingdom. At first, the king wouldn't hear of such a thing, but at last he agreed. As for the youngest lad, Ambrose, he did not even dare ask his father's permission to challenge the dragons.

In those days, there were only three dragons in the land. One had seven heads, the second had eight heads, and the third had nine heads. These three had devoured all the other dragons when they found that there were no more lads to eat. Andrew and Emerich joyfully galloped off toward the copper, silver and gold bridges that led to the the dragons' domain, while Ambrose stayed behind to console his royal father, who feared greatly for his other sons.

Now, Ambrose's godmother was a fairy, and because it was the custom for godmothers to give presents to their godchildren, Ambrose received from his fairy godmother a black egg with five corners. She placed the egg under Ambrose's left arm. Ambrose carried his egg about with him for seven winters and seven summers, and on Ash Wednesday of the eighth year, a horse with five legs and three heads jumped out of the egg. It was a magic horse—a Tátos—and could speak.

On the day that his two brothers went off to fight the dragons, Ambrose was thirteen years and thirteen days old, and his horse was exactly five years old. His two elder brothers had been gone some time when he went into the stable to his little horse, lay his head upon its neck, and began to weep bitterly. The little horse neighed loudly and asked, "Why are you crying, my dear master?" "Because," replied Ambrose, "I don't dare ask my father to let me go fight the dragons, although I want to so much."

"Go speak to your royal father, dear master, for he is suffering from a toothache. Tell him that the King of Herbs sends word to him through the Tátos horse that his toothache will not stop until he gives you permission. Tell him also that if he lets you go, there will soon be no more dragons left on this earth, but if you do not go, his two elder boys are certain to perish in the dragons' stomachs."

Thus spoke the Tátos colt, then it neighed so loudly that the whole world rang with the sound. Ambrose gave his father the horse's message, and still the king refused to let him go. But at last his toothache got the better of him, and after saying no for three straight hours, he reluctantly gave his word that if the Tátos horse could cure him, Ambrose could go and fight the dragons. No sooner had the king uttered these words than his toothache vanished.

Ambrose ran to tell the Tátos horse the good news, and the horse neighed with delight. "Fear nothing, my young master," the horse said, "for although our ride will be long, it will turn out well. Go to the crooked willow tree and fetch my great-great-grandmother's great-great-grandmother's saddle, and put it on me!" The prince rushed like a madman, fetched the old ragged saddle, and put it on his horse. Then the little horse asked him to plug up one of its nostrils. Ambrose did, and the horse blew upon him with the open nostril and— horror of horrors!—the prince became as dirty and mangy as a little piglet. The colt, however, turned into a horse with golden hair that glistened like a mirror. When the prince saw his reflection in the horse's coat, he became very sad.

"Plug up my other nostril," said the horse. At first Ambrose refused, but the horse neighed very loudly and, since it is always unwise to disobey the commands of a Tátos horse, the prince plugged up the horse's other nostril. The horse then opened wide its mouth and breathed upon the lad, who at once became a handsome prince. "Sit on my back, master," the horse said, "for now we are worthy of each other, and there is no danger in the world we cannot overcome. Just remember to do as I tell you, and listen to no one else."

In less than an hour, they arrived on the shore of the Red Sea, which flows into the Blue Sea, and there they saw a copper bridge. At the other side of the copper bridge lived the dragon with seven heads, and at the foot of the copper bridge stood an inn. Andrew and Emerich were already there, and they had begun to eat and drink. When they saw the handsome stranger entering the inn, the knives and forks dropped from the two princes' hands. They did not even suspect he was their brother, and when they learned that he, too, had come to fight the dragons, they quickly made friends with him. Andrew and Emerich had eaten too much, and were decidedly drunk, and so when night came they slept soundly. Ambrose ate little, drank nothing, and slept lightly.

At dawn the Tátos horse pulled his master's hair in order to wake him, for it knew that the dragon would be weakest at sunrise. Ambrose jumped on the horse's back and soon arrived at the copper bridge. The dragon rushed to meet them.

"Phew! I smell a strange smell," snorted the dragon. "Is that you, Ambrose? Are you and your mangy horse prepared to die?"

4

They fought for an hour or more, and then Ambrose, with two strokes, slashed off six of the dragon's heads. For a long time, he could not cut off the seventh, because all the dragon's magic power was in that head, but at last the seventh head fell beside the others. The dragon had seven horses, and Ambrose tied these together and led them to the inn, where he left them next to the horse of his brother, Emerich.

Andrew and Emerich did not awaken until nine o'clock. Then Ambrose told them how he had slain the dragon with seven heads, and taken away his seven horses, and given them to Emerich. The three continued their journey together as far as the silver bridge, where they found lodgings at another inn. Emerich and Andrew ate and drank and went to sleep as before. The Tátos horse awakened his master at daybreak. Ambrose dressed quickly and rode off, while his two brothers slept like babies.

The Tátos horse smelled the dragon ten miles off, and growled like a dog. The dragon threw sparks at Ambrose, and they met with a tremendous clash on the bridge. It was not an easy fight, but at last, helped by the skilful movements of his horse, Ambrose cut off the dragon's eight heads. Then he took the beast's eight horses and tied them to a post near the horse of his brother Andrew.

When Andrew and Emerich awoke around noon, they were delighted to find eight splendid horses, and guessed at once that the strange prince must have killed the eight-headed dragon, for they had never before seen horses quite like these. Ambrose urged them to hurry on and kill the third dragon, and so they all rode to the foot of a golden bridge, where once again they found lodging at an inn. But Andrew and Emerich had too much to eat and drink, and so they were snoring peacefully the next morning when Ambrose rode off on his horse.

Ambrose met the dragon with nine heads on the golden bridge, and though they fought long and fiercely, neither one could conquer the other. The dragon suggested that Ambrose change himself into a steel hoop, while he became a hoop of flint, and that they both climb to the top of a nearby mountain that nearly touched the sun, and roll down in two tracks. If the flint hoop left the track and struck sparks against the steel hoop, Ambrose's head would fall off, but if the steel hoop left the track and struck the flint hoop, all the dragon's nine heads would fall off. But Ambrose and the dragon each rolled straight down the mountain without touching the other.

Then the dragon proposed another contest to Ambrose. "I will become a red flame and you will become a white one, and the flame that burns brightest shall win." Ambrose agreed, and the contest began. Then they heard a crow croaking inside a hollow tree. Now, this crow was an old friend of the dragon, and the dragon asked it to please bring a beakful of water and put out the white flame. In return the dragon promised he would give the crow Ambrose's flesh to eat. Ambrose asked the crow for just a single drop of water, and promised the crow the dragon's huge body in return. The crow filled its crop with water and spat it over the red flame, giving Ambrose the victory.

Ambrose led the dragon's nine horses to the inn, where his brothers were still snoring loudly, even though it was well past noon. He gave them the nine horses and said goodbye.

Then Ambrose changed himself into a rabbit and ran over hill and dale until he came to a house where the dragons' wives were talking together. The wife of the dragon with seven heads picked up the rabbit and petted it, saying, "I don't know if Ambrose killed my husband, but if he did, I will change into a pear tree and my fruit will be smelled seven miles off, and though the pears be sweet to the taste, they will be deadly poison and will bring a plague to the world that will not end until Ambrose sinks his sword into the tree."

Then the wife of the dragon with the eight heads took the little rabbit in her lap, and said, "If Ambrose has killed my husband, I will change myself into a spring, and there will be eight streams flowing out of this spring, and each one will run for eight miles and then divide into eight more streams. And whoever drinks from them will die, and the poisonous water will only cease to flow when Ambrose washes his sword in it."

Then the wife of the dragon with nine heads took the rabbit and said, "If Ambrose killed my husband, I will become a bramble that will spread along all the roads of the world, and whoever trips over me will die. But if Ambrose cuts my stalk anywhere, the bramble will dry up everywhere."

Then the little rabbit scampered off, but the mother of the three wives—an old woman with an iron nose—chased it over hill and dale. Finally

Ambrose outran her. Then he changed back into his own shape, and caught up with his two brothers.

As the three of them traveled, they became hungry. They smelled the sweet scent of pears on the breeze, and soon came to a pear tree. Ambrose sprang from his horse, ran to the tree, and plunged his sword into the roots. Blood seeped from the tree, and he thought he heard a voice moaning. Onward they went, and they began to grow thirsty. Emerich saw a spring and ran toward it, but Ambrose ran faster and got there before him. He washed his sword in the spring, and horrible screams arose from the water as it disappeared. Ambrose saddled his horse and galloped onward, searching for the bramble that must be spreading across the land. When he found it, he cut it in two, and with a cry of pain the bramble vanished. Ambrose sent his horse home with his brothers, and went his way alone.

The old woman with the iron nose was still chasing Ambrose, and now she drove a carriage pulled by two cats. Near the edge of a forest she caught him. Imagine his surprise when she began to flirt with him as if she were a young girl! Ambrose kicked at the carriage, but his foot stuck to the axle. Then the two cats bounded on over hill and dale, dragging him with them, until suddenly the carriage descended into the earth and stopped.

Then the old woman with the iron nose asked Ambrose if he would agree to marry her. Ambrose would not! "Very well," said the woman. "Off to prison you shall go, with twelve hundred pounds of iron to bind you!"

Nine servants seized hold of Ambrose and dragged him nine miles down into the earth. They fastened an iron weight to his feet, and secured it with a lock. The poor lad wept and groaned, but no one heard him except a pretty serving girl, who began to visit Ambrose in secret. He promised to marry her if she could help him escape. "You will never get out of this place," the girl told him, "unless you marry the old woman with the iron nose. Then will she reveal all her secrets, and tell you how you may do away with her." So Ambrose sent word to the old woman that he had changed his mind and wanted to marry her.

After the wedding, Ambrose asked, "What keeps you alive for so long, my love? As your husband, I want to protect you and keep you from harm." At first, the old woman wouldn't tell him, but he kissed and flattered her so much that finally she revealed her secret. "I keep a wild boar in the meadow yonder," she said, "and inside the boar is a hare, and inside the hare is a pigeon, and inside the pigeon is a tiny box, and inside the box are two beetles, one dark and one bright. The bright beetle holds my life and the black beetle holds my power."

When the old woman went for a drive in her carriage, as she did each day, Ambrose found the the wild boar, and took out the hare. From the hare he took the pigeon, from the pigeon he took the box, and from the box he took the two beetles. He killed the black one, but kept the shining one in his hand. The old woman's power left her at once and she returned home, for she felt her death was near.

"If I should die," she told Ambrose, "you must take my golden wand from the closet and strike it against the side of my castle, and the castle will become a golden apple. The two cats will carry you back to your own world." Ambrose listened. Then he crushed the shining beetle.

Ambrose found the golden wand and tapped the side of the castle with it and it turned into a golden apple. He asked the serving girl to sit beside him in the carriage, and he harnessed the two cats and touched them with the golden wand. In a flash they arrived in the upper world. Many years before, the old woman had kidnapped the girl from her father, who was king of the land where the entrance to the underground was found. Ambrose set the golden apple on a hilltop, tapped it with the rod, and it turned into a beautiful castle again.

Ambrose married his sweetheart and lived with her in the castle. Later, he returned to his father's land, where he found that many strong youths had grown up in the years since the last dragons had been destroyed. The old king divided his kingdom among his three sons, giving the best part to Ambrose, who took his father to live with him and kept him in great honor. Ambrose and his wife had pretty children, who loved to ride every day on the Tátos horse.

Fair Angiola

[ITALY]

nce upon a time there were seven women who lived near the house of a witch, and the witch had a garden that was surrounded by a high wall and guarded by a talking donkey. The seven women were overcome with a longing to eat the jujube fruits which grew in the witch's garden, and so they went there secretly at night and gave the donkey some nice soft grass. While he was eating, they filled their aprons with jujubes and left without the witch seeing them. They did this many times, until at last the witch couldn't help but notice that she had far fewer jujubes than before. She asked the donkey if he had seen anyone, but he answered no, he had seen no one. That night, the witch dug a deep hole in the garden, got inside, and covered herself with leaves and branches. The seven women came and were picking jujubes when one of them noticed the witch's long ear sticking out from the leaves and branches. Thinking it was a mushroom, the woman tried to pick it.

The witch jumped out of the hole and ran after the women until she caught one of them. The poor woman cried and begged for mercy, saying she would never come to the garden again. Finally the witch agreed to let her go, but on one condition. The woman would give the witch the child she was carrying, whether it be a boy or girl, when it reached the age of seven. The woman promised, and the witch released her.

Not long afterward, the woman had a beautiful baby girl named Angiola. When Angiola was six years old, her mother sent her to school to learn to sew and knit, and every day on her way to school, the girl had to walk by the witch's garden. One day, when she was almost seven, Angiola came face to face with the witch herself. The witch smiled, and offered Angiola some fruit, and said, "Angiola, I am your aunt. Tell your mother you have seen me, and that she should not forget her promise."

Angiola ran home and told her mother, and her mother said, "When you see your aunt again, tell her you have forgotten to give me her message." Days passed, and the witch was always waiting for Angiola as she walked to school, and always asking for her mother's reply, but Angiola just kept saying she had forgotten to ask.

At last the witch became angry. "Since you are so forgetful, I must help you remember," she said, and she bit Angiola's little finger very hard. Poor Angiola ran home crying. Then her mother knew that she must keep her promise and give the girl to the witch. So when Angiola left for school the next morning her mother said, "Tell your aunt to do whatever she thinks is best for you." When Angiola repeated these words to her, the witch said, "Come with me now, for you are mine."

The witch took her to a tower that had no door, but only one small window at the top. There Angiola lived with the witch, and the witch treated her kindly, as if she were her own child. And whenever the witch would arrive home, she would stand under the window of the tower and say,

> *Angiola,*
> *Fair Angiola,*
> *Let down your hair.*

Then Angiola would let down her long shining hair and pull the witch up.

One day, when Angiola had grown to be a tall and beautiful maiden, a king's son was out hunting and he happened to ride near her tower. He was surprised to see this strange house without a door, and he wondered how anyone got in or out. Just then the old witch arrived, and stood beneath the window, and called,

> *Angiola,*
> *Fair Angiola,*
> *Let down your hair.*

Angiola's beautiful hair tumbled down, and the witch climbed up. The prince was pleased to know this secret. He hid nearby until the witch was gone. Then he stood beneath the window and called,

Angiola,
Fair Angiola,
Let down your hair.

Then Angiola let down her hair, thinking that it was the witch calling to her. When a strange man appeared at the window, she was frightened. But the prince spoke to her kindly and gently. He begged her to escape with him and become his wife, and at last Angiola agreed.

Angiola didn't want the witch to know where she had gone, so she gave a bit of food to every chair and table and cupboard in the house. They were all living beings and might easily betray her. Unfortunately, she did not see the broom that was hidden behind the door, and she gave it nothing. Then Angiola took a bar of soap, a towel and a nail from the witch's chamber and hurried off with the prince. The witch's little dog, who loved Angiola, ran along beside them.

Not long afterwards, the witch returned and called up to Angiola as she always did. But no matter how many times she called, Angiola's hair did not tumble down, so at last the witch had to go and fetch a tall ladder and use it to climb up to the window. When she saw that Angiola was gone, she asked the tables and chairs and cupboards what had happened, and each one said, "I don't know." Then the broom cried out from the corner, "Angiola has run off with the king's son, who is going to marry her!"

The witch flew into a rage and ran after them as fast as she could. When she had nearly caught up with them, Angiola threw down the soap, and it changed into a great, tall, slippery mountain, and each time the witch tried to climb it, she would slide back down again. But finally she got over it, and began chasing them again. Then Angiola threw down the nail, and it became a great forest of nails, and the witch had to struggle to get through it, and she scratched and cut herself. When Angiola saw that the witch had almost caught up with them a third time, she threw down the towel, and it became a wide raging river, and the witch tried to swim across. But as she swam, the river grew wider, and wider, and wider, and finally she had to give up. In her anger, the witch cursed Angiola, saying, "May your face become the face of a dog!" And it did.

The prince was very sorrowful. "How can I take you home to my parents?" he asked. "When they see you, they will never allow us to marry." So he led Angiola to a little house where she was to live until the evil enchantment was lifted. He returned to the palace alone, and visited Angiola whenever he went hunting. Often she wept over her misfortune, until one day the little dog that had followed her from the witch's house said, "Do not weep, Angiola. I will go to the witch and beg her to remove the spell."

The little dog ran to the witch's house, and jumped into her lap and licked her hands and face. "Angiola sends you her greeting," the dog told her. "She wants you to know that she is very sad, for she cannot go to the palace with her dog's face, and cannot marry the prince."

"That serves her right for leaving me," said the witch. "She can keep her dog's face!"

But the dog begged very hard, and told her that Angiola had suffered enough already, and so at last the witch gave him a little flask of water. "Take this to Angiola," she said. "Tell her to wash with it, and she will become beautiful once again."

The dog thanked the witch and hurried off with the flask. He carried it to Angiola, and as soon as she washed in the water, her dog's face vanished and she became even more beautiful than before. The prince escorted her to the palace, and the king and queen welcomed her. They gave Angiola and the prince a splendid wedding, and they all lived happily ever after.

The Wild Man

[SWEDEN]

A king once lived who knew of no greater pleasure than the hunt. Early and late he hunted with hawk and hound and he always brought home meat for the table. But one day there was no game to be found anywhere. The king was about to return home empty-handed when suddenly he spied a creature running through the trees. The king put spurs to his horse and chased after it, and to his great surprise he caught a wild man, as ugly as a troll, with hair like shaggy moss. Whatever words the king would say to him, the wild man would not answer. This made the king angry, and he ordered his servants to keep a close watch over the wild man and not let him escape. Now, in those times it was the custom for the king and his men to sit up late drinking and making merry, and that evening was just such an occasion. The king lifted his drinking horn, and asked, "What do you think of our hunt today? Have we ever before failed to bring back meat for the table?"

The men answered that there had never been a hunter the equal of the king. Hadn't he brought home a wild beast no one had ever seen before? This praise pleased the king, and he asked what they thought he should do with the wild man. One of the courtiers answered, "You should keep him here in the palace, so that the world knows what a great hunter you are. But lock him up, and take care not to let him escape, for he is sly and crafty."

The king sat silent for a spell, then raised his horn. "I will do as you say, and I vow that if anyone lets the wild man escape, that person shall die, even if it be my own son." Then the king emptied his drinking horn, so that his oath could not be broken. His courtiers were uneasy. They had never heard the king speak in this way, and they could plainly see that the drink had gone to his head.

Next morning, the king ordered that a cage be built near the palace, secured by iron locks and bars, with only one small window for passing food and drink to the prisoner. Then the wild man was put in the cage, and only the king himself had the keys. There the wild man sat, still and speechless, day and night, and people came and stared at him. Time passed, and war broke out, and the king was obliged to go and fight. On the evening before his departure, he gave the queen the keys to the wild man's cage, and made her promise that the prisoner would not escape.

Now, the king and queen had an only child, a young prince. The boy was wandering in the palace one day when he came to the wild man's cage. He sat beside the cage and played with his favorite toy, a golden apple. It happened that the prince tossed the golden apple through the window of the cage, and the wild man threw it out again. The boy thought this was a fine game, and he threw the apple into the cage again, and the wild man threw it back, and so they played for some time. But at length pleasure turned to sorrow. The wild man kept the apple and would not throw it back. The little prince threatened the wild man, then pleaded with him, then burst into tears.

"It was wrong of your father to make me his prisoner," the wild man said to him, "and you will not get your apple back unless you promise to help me regain my freedom."

"Yes, I promise. Just give me back my golden apple," begged the prince.

"Go to your mother. Ask her to comb your hair, and wait for a chance to take the keys from her belt. Then come and open the door. Afterwards, return the keys to her using the same trick, and no one will be the wiser."

So the boy took the keys from his mother, and then he let the wild man out of his cage. As they parted, the wild man said, "Here is your golden apple as I promised. I will always be grateful to you for helping me escape, and I will help you one day when you are in need." Then he ran away.

News of the wild man's escape soon spread throughout the palace, and the queen sent the royal guards to search the town, the fields and the woods, but no trace of him was found. Time passed, and the queen grew frightened, for she expected her husband to return at any time.

At last the king arrived, and his first question was whether they had taken good care of the wild man when he was away. Then the queen had to tell him that his prisoner had escaped. The king was furious. He ordered that everyone in the kingdom be questioned, but it seemed that no one knew a thing about it. Finally the little prince confessed that he had set the wild man free.

The queen grew deadly pale, then after a long silence the king spoke. "Never shall it be said that I broke my vow, even for the sake of my own flesh and blood." He ordered his men to take the prince into the forest, to slay him, and to bring back his heart as proof.

There was great sorrow in the kingdom, for the prince was everyone's favorite, but the king's word was law, and his servants took the prince deep into the forest. There they met a man herding pigs, and one of the servants said, "It isn't right to lay violent hands upon this child. Let us buy a pig from this man, and take its heart back to the king instead. Who will know the difference?" The others thought this was a good idea, and so they bought a pig, slaughtered it, and took out its heart. They told the prince to go far away and never return.

The prince wandered on, eating the nuts and wild berries that grew in the forest, until he came to a mountain, and on top of the mountain stood a tall fir tree. "I may as well climb up that tree," he said to himself, "and see whether there is any path out of the forest." No sooner said than done. When he reached the top of the tree, and looked around, he spied a great palace far in the distance.

He climbed down from the tree and hurried toward the palace. On his way he met a farm boy who was happy to trade clothes with him, so that when the prince came to the palace, he looked like a peasant lad, and he was hired to herd the king's cattle. He worked hard, and grew tall and handsome.

Now, the princess of that country was fair and kind and courteous, and any man would have been happy to marry her. Princes came from near and far to ask for her hand, but she refused every one of them. Even so, more suitors came every day, until at last her father grew tired of saying no to all of them. He went to visit the princess in her bower and demanded that she choose a husband, but she would not. Her father grew desperate, and threatened to make the choice himself. Then the princess declared that the only man she would take as her husband would be the one who could ride a horse, fully armed, to the top of a glass mountain.

The king sent out a proclamation, and when the appointed day came, the princess sat on a throne at the top of the mountain, with a golden crown on her head and a golden apple in her hand, and she was so radiant that anyone who saw her would joyfully have risked his life for her.

The suitors assembled, riding noble horses and dressed in armor that shone like fire, and from every part of the world people flocked in countless multitudes to watch the contest. Trumpets were sounded as the suitors galloped up the mountain, one after another. But the mountain was slippery and steep. One after another the suitors and their horses tumbled headlong downward, and the thunderous crashing of their armor could be heard for miles around.

The prince was busy tending the king's cattle when he heard the noise, and he sat down on a stone and wept, wishing that he could be among the riders. Then he heard footsteps behind him. He turned and saw his old friend, the wild man.

"You are lonely and sad," said the wild man.

"I have reason to be," the prince replied. "Because of you I was driven away from my home. Now I do not have a horse or armor, and so I cannot ride to the glass mountain and compete for the hand of the princess."

"You helped me in my time of need," said the wild man. "Now it is my turn to help you." He led the prince to a cave deep in the earth where he found a suit of armor, forged of the hardest steel, and so bright that it shed a blue light all around, and it fit him perfectly. Nearby stood a powerful horse, saddled and bridled, scraping the ground with its steel-shod hooves, and champing at the bit.

"Arm yourself quickly," the wild man said. "Then go try your luck. I will watch the cattle for you while you are gone."

The prince quickly armed himself and buckled spurs on his heels. He felt as light in the steel armor as a bird in the air, and he sprang into the saddle and rode at full speed to the foot of the glass mountain. The hapless suitors had all given up for the day when a young knight appeared, clad in steel from head to foot, with a shield on his arm and a sword in his belt, and he carried himself so nobly in the saddle that he was a pleasure to behold.

Everyone asked who he was, for no one had seen him before, but they had little time to wonder. The knight raised himself in the stirrups, set spurs to his horse, and shot like an arrow straight up the glass mountain. But when he was about halfway up, he suddenly turned his horse, rode back down, and disappeared into the forest.

Early the next morning, the suitors gathered for a second assault on the mountain. Once again the prince was watching the king's cattle, sad and sorrowful. The wild man appeared as before and led the prince to the cave, where he found a suit of armor just his size made of the brightest silver. A snow white horse stood pawing the ground and champing the bit with excitement. The prince put on the armor, mounted the horse, and galloped away. Once again, he rode full speed up the glass mountain. But when he had almost reached the top, he nodded to the princess, then turned, rode down the mountain and disappeared.

The same happened on the third day, except that this time the prince wore armor of pure gold, and he rode all the way to the top of the mountain where he dismounted, bowed before the princess, and received the golden apple from her hand. Then he sped down the mountain and disappeared into the forest.

The crowd shouted for joy. Trumpets and horns were sounded, and the king proclaimed that the knight in the golden armor had won the hand of the princess. All that now remained was to find the victorious knight, for no one knew who he was. The princess, meanwhile, grew pale and thin, and was pining away with love, while the other suitors murmured in discontent. The king commanded that every young man in the country must appear at the palace. When they were all gathered, the princess noticed a man standing at the edge of the crowd. He was wrapped in a gray cloak like those worn by herdsmen, with the hood drawn up over his head so that one could scarcely see his face. Yet the princess recognized him instantly. She ran towards him, pulled down the hood, and clasped him in her arms. "Here he is!" she shouted, and everyone began to laugh when they saw that she had chosen the king's herding boy.

"Good gracious!" cried the king. "Must I have a lowly cow herd for a son-in-law?"

"You deserve a king's son as a son-in-law," said the herding boy, and he threw aside the gray cloak. There stood a handsome young prince clad in gold from head to foot, and in his hand was the golden apple.

Now he was recognized by one and all as the knight who had ridden up the glass mountain. The king ordered preparations for the wedding, and a banquet was given such as has never been seen before or since. Thus did the prince gain the king's daughter and half the kingdom. And when the feasting had lasted seven days, the prince took his bride to his father's kingdom, where the king and queen wept with joy to see him alive. They lived happily ever after, of course, and the wild man was never seen again.

Tatterhood

[NORWAY]

here lived a king and a queen once upon a time who had no children, and this caused them much sadness. The queen scarcely had one happy hour, for she was constantly thinking how dreary and lonesome her life was in the palace. "If only we had children, it would be so much nicer here," she sighed. Then one day a ragged beggar lassie came to the palace and claimed that her own mother knew of a way for the queen to get a child. At first the queen did not believe her, but the lassie insisted, and so the queen sent her to fetch her mother. "Do you know what your daughter said?" the queen asked the beggar woman when she came into the room. "No," the woman replied. "She told me that you can get me children if you wish," answered the queen. "Queens shouldn't listen to beggar lassies' silly tales," said the woman, and she strode haughtily out of the room.

Then the queen became angry, but the young lassie told her she must try again, and this time she should offer the beggar woman her finest food and drink. The queen was willing to do that, and so the lassie's mother was fetched again, and this time she was served a meal fit for royalty. Again the queen asked if she could help her. "I know of one way," the woman told her. "In the evening before you go to bed, have two basins of water brought to you. Wash yourself in each one, and afterwards throw the water under the bed. Next morning you will find two flowers growing there, the one fair, the other foul. You must eat the fair flower, but do not even touch the foul flower. Whatever you do, be sure not to forget that last part!"

So the queen did as the beggar woman told her. She had the water brought up in two basins, and washed herself in them, then emptied them under the bed afterwards. The next morning, she found two flowers growing there, and one was very bright and lovely, but the other was dank and withered. She ate the lovely flower at once, and it tasted so sweet that she just couldn't help herself. She ate the foul flower as well.

In time the queen was brought to childbed and she gave birth to a girl who was all gray and loathly, and what was even more strange, the baby could walk and speak from the very first.

"Mama! Mama!" the baby cried.

"Heaven protect me if *I* am your mama!" said the queen.

"Don't worry, mama," said the baby. "Soon you will have another daughter who is prettier than I, and she will be your heart's desire. As for me, I will be a wild princess!"

Then the baby toddled downstairs and into the courtyard, where she climbed onto the back of a goat. She rode the goat right into the kitchen and grabbed a wooden spoon from the astonished cook.

The queen then gave birth to that one's twin, and the second girl was as fair and sweet a baby as anyone had ever set eyes on. They called the elder twin Tatterhood, because she was so ragged, and because she wore a hood which hung about her ears in tatters. The queen could scarcely bear to look at her, and the nurses tried to lock her away in a secret room. But it was no use, for the younger twin could not bear to be without her wild sister.

Time passed, and the girls grew to be young women. One winter's evening, there was a frightful noise and clatter outside in the courtyard. The queen told them that this was a pack of trolls and witches that sometimes came to the palace at Christmas time. Tatterhood swore that she would drive them off, though everyone warned her to let the invaders alone. Tatterhood rode out on her goat, brandishing her wooden spoon, but before she left, she begged the queen to make sure all the palace doors were shut tight while she was gone.

Tatterhood attacked the trolls and witches, and the sound of the battle was terrible to hear. The whole palace creaked and groaned as if every joint and beam were going to be torn out of place. Now it happened that one door did get slightly ajar, and Tatterhood's sister peeked out to see how things were going. Then up came an old witch and whisked off her head and stuck a calf's head on her shoulders in its place. The princess ran back into the great hall on all fours, mooing pitifully.

When the trolls had all been driven off, and Tatterhood returned and saw what had happened to her sister, she became angry and scolded everyone for not keeping better watch. "Now I shall have to see that she gets her own head back," said Tatterhood, and she asked the king to prepare a ship for her. She would take along neither captain nor crew, but insisted upon sailing away with only her sister and herself, and the king and queen had to let her have her own way.

Tatterhood sailed long and far until the ship arrived in the land where the trolls and witches lived. She steered the ship to shore and told her sister to stay below deck while she herself rode her goat to the witches' castle. She found one of the windows open, and, looking inside, she saw her sister's head hanging beside the window. She snatched it up quickly and galloped off.

The witches came howling after her, and they were as thick and as angry as a swarm of bees. The goat snorted and puffed and butted at them with his horns, and Tatterhood beat and banged them about with her wooden spoon, and so the witches had to give up. Tatterhood got back to her ship, and took the calf's head off her sister, and replaced it with her own head. Then the two of them sailed a long, long way to a strange kingdom.

Now, the king of that land was a widower, as Tatterhood knew well, and he had an only son. When the king saw a strange ship arrive, he sent messengers down to the strand to find out whence it came, and who owned it. When the king's men arrived, the only person they saw aboard the ship was Tatterhood, riding her goat around the deck at full speed with her hair streaming in the wind. The messengers were amazed at this sight, and asked wasn't there anyone else on board. Yes, said Tatterhood, she had a sister. And though the messengers wanted to see the sister, Tatterhood refused. "No one shall see her unless the king comes himself," she said, and began to gallop about on her goat until the deck thundered.

When the king's men reported what they had seen and heard, the king set out at once to see the strange lassie who rode on a goat. When he got there, Tatterhood led her sister forth, and she was so fair and gentle that the king fell head and ears in love with her on the spot. He escorted both of them to the palace, and wanted to have the sister for his queen, but Tatterhood refused unless the king's son agreed to marry her. You may imagine that the prince was not eager to do this, so terribly wild and ugly was Tatterhood, but at last the king talked him into it. He promised to marry her, though it went against his will, and he was sad and heavy-hearted.

Preparations were made for a grand wedding, with brewing and baking, and when everything was ready, the bridal party were to go to church. First the king drove off in a carriage with his bride, and she was so lovely that all the people stared at her until she was out of sight. After them came the prince riding on horseback beside Tatterhood, who trotted along on her goat with her wooden spoon in her hand. And the prince looked as if he was going to a burial, not to his own wedding.

"Why don't you say something?" Tatterhood asked when they had ridden a bit.

"What should I say?" said the prince.

"Well, you might ask me why I ride upon this ugly goat," said Tatterhood.

"Why *do* you ride on that ugly goat?" asked the prince.

"Is it an ugly goat? Why, I believe it's the grandest horse that a bride ever rode upon," said Tatterhood. And in a trice the goat became a horse, the finest the prince had ever set eyes on.

They rode on a bit further, but the prince was just as sad as before, and couldn't get a word out. Tatterhood asked him again why he didn't talk, and the prince answered that he didn't know what to talk about.

"You could ask me why I ride with this ugly spoon in my fist."

"Why *do* you ride with that ugly spoon?" asked the prince.

"Is it an ugly spoon? Why, I believe it's the loveliest silver wand a bride ever wished for," said Tatterhood, and in an instant it became a silver wand, so dazzling bright that sunbeams seemed to glisten from it.

On they rode, and the prince was every bit as sorrowful as before, and he never said a word. Then Tatterhood asked him again why he didn't speak, and bade him ask why she wore that ugly gray hood on her head.

"Why *do* you wear that ugly gray hood on your head?" asked the prince.

"Is it an ugly hood? I believe it's the brightest golden crown a bride ever wore," answered Tatterhood, and it became a crown on the spot.

Then they rode for a long while, and again the prince was so woeful that he sat without speaking a word. His bride asked him why he didn't talk, and bade him ask why her face was so ugly and ashen gray.

"Why *is* your face so ugly and ashen gray?"

"Am I ugly?" asked the bride. "You think my sister is pretty, but I am ten times prettier." And when the prince looked at her, she was.

They drank the bridal cup both deep and long, and after that, the prince and the king and their brides traveled to the land of the princesses' father and mother, and they held another bridal feast. There was no end of fun, and if you hurry and run to the palace, you may still find something left in the bridal cup for you.

The Thirteenth Son
of the King of Ireland

[IRELAND]

ong ago a king lived in Ireland who had thirteen sons, and as they grew up he taught them every art and knowledge befitting their rank. One day the king went hunting, and saw a swan swimming in a lake with thirteen little ones. She kept driving away the thirteenth, and would not let it come near the others. The king wondered greatly at this, and when he came home he summoned his old blind sage and said, "I saw a great wonder today while out hunting. A swan had thirteen cygnets, and she drove the thirteenth away from her, keeping the other twelve by her side. Why should a mother hate her thirteenth little one, and guard the other twelve?"

"All creatures on earth, whether beast or human, that have thirteen children should put the thirteenth out and let it find its own destiny," said the old blind sage. "Now, you have thirteen sons, and it seems you must offer the thirteenth to fate."

"But how can I give one of them away when I am so fond of all of them? And which one should it be?" asked the king.

"When the thirteen come home tonight, shut the door against the last that comes."

Now the eldest lad, Sean, was the best, the hero of them all, but that night it happened that he came home last, and when he arrived, he found that his father had shut the door against him.

"Father, what are you doing?" cried Sean.

"It is my duty," said the king, "to give one of my sons to fate, and it must be you."

"Well, then, at least give me a good horse for the road," said Sean, and his father gave him a black steed that could overtake the wind. Sean mounted the steed and hurried off. He rode each day without resting, and at night he slept in the woods. One morning, Sean put on some old clothes which he had in a pack, and leaving his horse in the woods, he walked along the road. It was not long before a king rode up and stopped before him.

"Who are you and where are you going?" the king asked.

"Oh," said Sean, "I have lost my way. I don't know where to go or what to do."

"I'll tell you what," said the king. "Come with me, for I have a great many cows, and I have no one to watch them. And I am in terrible trouble. My daughter will soon die a horrible death."

"How will she die?" asked Sean.

"There is a great serpent of the sea that must devour a king's daughter every seven years. Once in seven years this beast comes up out of the sea for its meal. The turn now has fallen to my own daughter, yet we don't know what day the serpent will appear. All of us in the whole castle are in mourning for my poor child."

"Perhaps someone will save her," said Sean.

"Oh, there is a whole army of kings' sons who have come, and they all promise to save her, but I'm afraid none of them can conquer the sea serpent."

Sean agreed to go with the king and to serve him for seven years. The next morning, the lad drove the king's cows out to pasture. Now, there were three giants living not far from the king. They lived in three castles in sight of each other, and every night each of these giants shouted just before going to bed. So loud was each giant's shout that people heard it all over the country.

Sean drove the cattle up to one giant's land, and pushed down the wall around his pasture, and let the animals go in. The grass was very high there, and three times better than any in the king's pastures. As Sean sat watching the cattle, the giant came running towards him, crying, "I don't know whether to put a pinch of you in my nose or a bite of you in my mouth, you tiny rascal!"

"Bad luck to me," said Sean, "if I didn't come here to take the life out of you!"

"How would you like to fight me, on the gray stones, or with sharp swords?" asked the giant.

"I'll fight you on the gray stones," said Sean, "where your great legs will be sinking down and mine standing high."

They faced one another and began to fight,

and at the first encounter the giant sank in the gray stones up to his knees. At the second, he sank in up to his waist, and at the third, up to his shoulders.

"Come and help me out of here," cried the giant, "and I'll give you my castle and all I have. I'll give you my sword of light that never fails to kill at a blow. I'll give you my black horse that can overtake the wind."

Then Sean killed the giant and went up to the castle, where the giant's housekeeper said to him, "Oh, it's welcome you are if you have killed the wicked giant that lives here. Come with me and I'll show you all his riches and treasures."

She opened the door of the giant's storeroom and said, "All this is yours, and here are the keys of the castle."

"Keep them till I come again," said Sean, "and wake me in the evening." Then he lay down on the giant's bed.

Sean slept till evening, and then the house-keeper roused him. He drove the king's cattle home, and the cows never gave so much milk before in a week as they gave that night.

Sean asked the king if the serpent had come.

"Not today," said the king.

The king knew nothing of the strength of Sean, who was bare-footed, ragged and shabby.

The second morning Sean put the king's cows on the second giant's land. Out came the second giant with the same questions and threats as the first, and Sean spoke as on the day before.

They fell to fighting, and when the giant was up to his shoulders in the hard gray rocks, he said,

"I'll give you my brown horse and my sword of light if you'll spare my life."

"Where is your sword of light?" asked Sean.

"It is hung up over my bed."

Sean ran to the giant's castle, and took the sword, which screamed out when he seized it. But he held it fast, hurried back to the giant and asked, "How shall I test the edge of this sword?"

"Against a stick," was the reply.

"I see no stick better than your own neck," said Sean, and he swept the head off the giant.

Sean went back to the castle and hung up the sword. "Blessings on you," said the housekeeper. "You have killed the giant! Come now, and I will show you his riches and treasures, which are now yours to keep."

Sean found more treasure in this castle than in the first one. When he had seen it all, he gave the keys to the housekeeper till he should need them again. He slept as on the day before, and he drove the cows home in the evening.

"I have had such good fortune since you came to work for me," the king said. "My cows gave three times as much milk today as they did yesterday."

"Well," said Sean, "have you any news of the serpent?"

"He didn't come today," said the king, "but he may come tomorrow."

The next day, Sean went out with the cows, and drove them to the fields of the third giant, who came and fought a more desperate battle than the other two. But Sean pushed him down among the gray rocks to his shoulders and killed him.

At the third castle, Sean was greeted with great joy by the housekeeper, who showed him the giant's treasures and gave him the keys, but he left the keys with her till he should have need of them. And that evening, the king's cows gave more milk than ever before.

On the fourth day, when Sean went out with the cows, he stopped at the first giant's castle. The housekeeper brought out the giant's clothes, which were black as night. Sean put on the giant's clothes, and girded on his sword of light. Then he mounted the black-haired steed which overtook the wind before and outstripped the wind behind. Rushing on between earth and sky, he never stopped till he came to the beach. There he saw hundreds upon hundreds of kings' sons and champions who were anxious to save the king's daughter, but they were so frightened of the terrible sea serpent that they wouldn't go near. When he had seen the princess and all the trembling champions, Sean turned his black steed toward the castle.

"What is this I see on the shore?" he asked of the king.

"Haven't you heard, stranger, that a sea serpent is coming to destroy my daughter?" the king replied.

"No, I haven't heard any such thing," said the stranger, who then turned and disappeared.

Soon the black horseman was standing before the princess, who sat alone on a rock near the sea. As she looked at the stranger, she thought that he was the finest man on earth, and her heart was greatly cheered.

"Have you no one to save you?" he asked.

"No one."

"Will you let me lay my head on your lap till the serpent comes? Then wake me."

"Yes," she said.

He put his head on her lap and fell asleep. While he slept, the princess took three hairs from his head and hid them in her bosom. As soon as she had hidden them, she saw the serpent coming on the sea, as wide and tall as an island, sending water up to the sky as it moved. She awakened the stranger and he sprang to defend her.

The serpent came up on the shore, his mouth open wide, and the stranger said, "This woman is mine, not yours!"

Then, drawing his sword of light, he swept off the monster's head with one stroke. But the head rushed back to its place and grew on again.

In an instant the serpent turned and went back into the sea, but as he went, he said, "I'll be here again tomorrow, and I'll swallow the whole world before me as I come."

"Well," answered the stranger, "maybe someone will be here to stop you."

Sean rode off before the princess could stop him. He returned to the first giant's castle and put away his horse, clothes and sword. He slept on the giant's bed till evening, when the housekeeper woke him, and then he drove home the cows.

When Sean saw the king, he asked, "How has your daughter fared today?"

"Oh, there's many a man claiming to be the stranger in black, but my daughter isn't saved yet, for the serpent says he will come again tomorrow."

"Well, never fear. Perhaps another champion will come," said Sean.

The next morning Sean drove the king's cows to the land of the second giant and left them to feed. Then he went to the castle, where the housekeeper met him.

"Let the brown horse be brought," said Sean. "Let the giant's sword and clothing be made ready for me."

The beautiful blue clothing of the second giant was brought, and his sword of light. Sean put on the clothing and the sword and mounted the brown steed. He sped away between earth and sky three times more swiftly than the day before. He rode first to the seashore, where he saw the princes and champions far away, trembling in dread of the serpent.

"Is there no one to save you?" he asked the princess.

"No one."

"Let me lay my head on your lap, and when the serpent comes, wake me."

He put his head on her lap, and while he slept she took out the three hairs, compared them with his hair, and said to herself, "You are the man who was here yesterday."

When the serpent appeared, coming over the sea, the princess roused the stranger, who sprang up and hurried to the beach. The monster, moving at a greater speed and raising more water than on the day before, came with open mouth to land. Sean stood in his way, and with one blow of the giant's sword made two halves of the serpent. But the two halves rushed together again, and were one as before. Then the serpent turned to the sea again, and said as he went, "All the champions on earth won't save her tomorrow!"

Sean sprang to his steed and rode back to the castle, leaving the princess in despair at his going. She tore her hair and wept for the loss of the blue champion, the one man who had dared to save her.

Sean put on his old clothes, and drove home the cows as usual. The king told him, "A strange champion, all dressed in blue, saved my daughter today. But she is grieving her life away because he is gone."

"Well that is a small matter, since her life is safe," said Sean.

There was a feast for the whole kingdom that night at the king's castle, and gladness was on every face that the king's daughter was safe again.

The next day, Sean drove the cows to the third giant's pasture. He went to the castle and told the housekeeper to bring the giant's sword and clothing, and to have the red steed waiting at the door. The third giant's clothes had as many colors as there are in the sky, and his boots were made of blue glass. And when he was dressed and mounted on the red steed, Sean was the handsomest man in the world.

"The serpent will be so enraged this time that no arms can stop him," the housekeeper told him. "He will rise from the sea with three great swords coming out of his mouth, and he could cut to pieces and swallow the whole world if it stood before him in battle. There is only one way to conquer the beast, and I will show it to you. Take this brown apple, put it in your shirt, and when he comes rushing from the sea with open mouth, throw the apple down his throat, and the great sea serpent will melt away and die on the strand."

Sean rode on the red steed between earth and sky with thrice the speed of the day before. He saw the princess sitting on the rock alone, he saw the trembling kings' sons in the distance watching and waiting to see what would happen, and he saw the king hoping for someone to save his daughter. Then he went to the princess, and put his head on her lap. When he had fallen asleep, she took the three hairs from her bosom and said, "You are the man who saved me yesterday."

The serpent was not long in coming. The princess roused Sean, who sprang to his feet and went to the sea. The serpent arose, terrible to look upon, with a mouth big enough to swallow the world and three sharp swords coming out of it. When he saw Sean, he sprang at him with a roar, but Sean threw the apple into his mouth, and the beast fell helpless on the shore, where his body flattened out and melted away to a dirty jelly on the sand. Then Sean went to the princess and told her that the serpent would never trouble any man or woman again.

The princess ran and tried to cling to him, but he mounted the red steed and rushed off between earth and sky before she could stop him. But she held so firmly to one of the blue glass boots that Sean had to leave it in her hands.

When he drove the cows home that night, the king came out, and Sean asked, "What news of the serpent?"

"Oh," said the king, "I've had extraordinary luck since you came to me. Today, a champion wearing all the colors of the sky and riding a red steed destroyed the serpent, and my daughter is safe forever. But she is ready to kill herself because she hasn't got the man that saved her."

That night there was a feast in the castle such as no one had ever seen before. The hall was filled with princes and champions, and each one said, "I am the man who saved the princess!"

The king sent for the old blind sage and asked how he could find the man who had saved his daughter. The old blind sage said, "Send out word to all the world that your daughter intends to marry the man who put an end to the serpent, the man whose foot will fit in the blue glass boot."

Well, the king sent out word to all the world to come try on the boot. It was too large for some, too small for others. When all had failed, the old sage said, "All have tried the boot but Sean."

"Oh, he is always out tending the cows," said the king. "What would be the use in his trying?"

"No matter," said the old blind sage. "Let someone fetch him."

So the king himself went and fetched Sean, saying, "Come now and try on the glass boot."

"How can I, when I have work to do here?" Sean replied.

"Oh, never mind that. You'll be back soon enough," the king told him.

Sean stood in front of the castle, and he saw the princess sitting by the window of her upstairs chamber with the glass boot in her hand. At that instant, the boot flew through the air and went onto his foot by itself. The princess rushed downstairs and into the arms of Sean.

Then the king sent ships with messengers to all the kings and queens of the world to come to the wedding of his daughter and Sean the champion. After the wedding, Sean went with his bride to live in the kingdom of the giants, and left his father-in-law on his own land.

King Lindorm

[SWEDEN]

nce upon a time, a king and queen ruled over a great country, and they had all the wealth they could ever desire, and lived happily with each other. But as the years went by their hearts became heavy, for they had no children. One day an old woman came to the castle and asked to speak with the queen. The servants offered her a penny and told her to go away, but the woman insisted they tell the queen that someone wished to see her who could help with her secret sorrow. This message was taken to her majesty, who ordered that the old woman be brought in. "I know your sadness," the woman told her, "and I have come to help you. You wish to have a son, and you shall have two if you follow my instructions carefully. Tonight, after you have bathed, look under the tub and you will find two red onions. Peel them and eat them, and in due time your wish will be fulfilled."

The queen did as the woman told her, and after she had bathed, she found two red onions under the tub. Then she knew that the old woman had been something more than she appeared to be. In her happiness the queen gobbled up the first onion, skin and all, before she remembered the woman's instructions. Well, it was too late now for the first onion, but she carefully peeled the second onion before she ate it.

Afterwards, everything happened as the old woman had foretold, except that the first child born to the queen was a hideous lindorm—a serpent! No one saw this monster except her waiting woman, who carried it quickly into the forest and left it there. The second child was a lovely little prince.

There was joy in the palace and throughout the entire kingdom because of the beautiful baby prince. No one knew that the queen's first-born child was a lindorm that lay writhing in the wild forest. Time passed, and the king and the queen lived in happiness and prosperity until the prince was twenty years of age. Then his parents told him that he should travel to another kingdom to seek a bride, for they were beginning to grow old, and wanted to see their son married before they were laid in their graves. The prince had his horses harnessed to his golden chariot, and set out to find a bride. But when he came to the first crossroad, a huge and terrible lindorm lay across the path, and his horses froze in fear.

"Where are you going?" hissed the lindorm.

"That is not your business," said the prince. "I am the prince, and I go where I please."

"Turn back," said the lindorm, "for I know your errand, and you will not marry before I do."

The prince returned home and told the king and queen what had happened. They said that he should try again the following day, and see if he could get past the lindorm. The prince went out the next morning, but again he got no further than the first crossroads. The lindorm stopped him there in the same way as before. And the exact same thing happened on the third day.

When the king and queen heard this for the third time, they could think of no better plan than to invite the lindorm to the palace, and to find him a mate. They imagined that the lindorm would be satisfied with anyone they might give him, and that perhaps they would get some prisoner to be his bride. The lindorm came to the palace and received a bride of this kind, but in the morning, she lay torn to pieces. The same thing happened each time that the king and queen compelled any woman to be the bride of the lindorm, until at last there were no more prisoners to give him.

The story of the lindorm soon spread throughout the kingdom, and there was one woman who listened to it with great delight. Her husband had a daughter by his first wife who was beautiful, gentle and good. The second wife also had a daughter, a disagreeable and horrible young woman. Compared to her stepsister, she appeared even more wicked and awful, and everyone turned away from her in loathing. So when the stepmother heard that there was a lindorm in the king's palace that tore all of its brides to pieces, she went to the king and said that her stepdaughter longed to marry the lindorm. The king was delighted, and gave orders that the maiden be brought to the palace at once.

When the messengers arrived, the girl was terribly frightened, for she knew that her stepmother planned her death. She begged that she might be allowed to spend one more night in her father's house. This was granted her, and late that evening she went secretly to her mother's grave. There she prayed for her mother's advice. How long she lay by the grave and wept no one can tell, but finally she fell asleep and slept until the sun rose. Then she awoke, happy at heart, and set out willingly with the king's messengers.

When the maiden arrived at the palace, the sight of her filled everyone with pity. But she was cheerful and confident, and asked the queen for a bridal chamber that the lindorm had never used before. This she got, and then she asked the queen to have a pot of strong lye placed on the fire, and to have three new scrubbing brushes laid beside it. The queen commanded that this be done. Then the maiden dressed herself in seven clean white shifts, and was married to the lindorm.

When they were alone in the bridal chamber, the lindorm ordered her, "Shed a shift."

"Lindorm," said she, "shed your skin."

"No other bride has asked me to do that," said the lindorm in surprise.

"But *I* ask you," said she.

Then the lindorm began to writhe and groan, and he cast away his outer skin, which lay on the floor, hideous to behold. Then his bride took off one of her snow-white shifts and cast in on top of the lindorm's skin.

"Bride, shed a shift," said the lindorm.

"Lindorm, shed your skin," she replied, and so he had to do it.

With groaning and pain, he cast off one skin after another, and for each skin, the maiden threw off one of her shifts until there lay on the floor seven lindorm skins and six snow-white shifts. The seventh she still had on. The lindorm now lay before her as a formless, slimy mass, which she began to scrub with the lye and scrubbing brushes.

When she had nearly worn out the last of the three brushes, there stood before her the loveliest youth in the world. He thanked her for saving him from his enchantment, and told her that he was the king and queen's eldest son, the heir to the kingdom. He asked if she would keep the wedding promise she had made to the lindorm, and be his bride. To this she was well content to answer yes.

King Lindorm lived long and happily with his queen, and there are some who say that if they are not dead now, they are still living to this day.

Ivan Goroh and
Vasilisa Golden Tress

[RUSSIA]

nce there was a tsar who had two sons, and a daughter who was a great beauty. Because she had thick golden hair that fell to her feet, the girl was called Vasilisa Golden Tress. Twenty years did the tsarevna live in her chamber, and only her mother, her father, her brothers and her nurses had ever seen her. But word of her beauty had spread far and wide. Many tsars heard of her, and sent envoys to ask for her hand in marriage, and so at last the tsar announced that his daughter would choose her husband.

Vasilisa Golden Tress had many lovely gowns and jewels, but she was weary of remaining always in her chamber. When her father announced that she would marry, she begged him to let her go outside. "I have not yet seen the wide world," she said, "nor have I walked on the grass, or even seen your palace. Please let me go with my nurses and walk in your garden."

So the tsar said yes, and Vasilisa Golden Tress went down from the lofty chamber into the garden, and she picked blue flowers, and she stepped away from her nurses and companions. Then a mighty whirlwind swept through the garden, seized the princess, and carried her away over mountains, across deep rivers, through three kingdoms and into the castle of a dragon.

The nurses ran screaming to the palace and threw themselves at the feet of the tsar. "A whirlwind carried off your daughter," they cried, "and we did not see where it took her. Please do not punish us, for it was not our fault."

The tsar was sad and the tsar was angry, but he pardoned the nurses. The next morning, he told all the assembled suitors that his daughter had been carried off by the whirlwind. The suitors were furious, and they did not believe him. They rushed to the princess' chamber, but nowhere could they find her. The tsar gave them gifts from his treasury, then they mounted their horses, and said farewell, and returned to their own lands.

The two brave brothers of Vasilisa Golden Tress saw the tears of their father and mother, and they asked to go off in search of their sister.

"My dear sons," said the tsar, "where will you search for her?"

"We will go everywhere that a road lies, and everywhere that a bird flies, and perhaps we will find her," the brothers answered.

The tsar gave them his blessing. Their mother prepared them for the journey. They wept and they parted.

The two princes journeyed on. They traveled a year, they traveled two. They passed through three kingdoms, and they saw lofty blue mountains. Between these mountains were sandy plains, and there lay the land of the dragon. The princes asked everyone they met had they not heard of, had they not seen Vasilisa Golden Tress. And from everyone the answer was the same, "We have not seen her, we have not heard of her."

The princes came to a great town where they met a ragged old man, cross-eyed and lame, with a crutch and a bag—a beggar. The princes stopped and gave him a silver coin, and asked had he not seen, had he not heard of Vasilisa Golden Tress.

"Ah, my friends," said the man, "it is clear you are strangers here. Our king, the dragon, has forbidden us to speak to strangers. He does not allow us to tell how a whirlwind bore the beautiful princess past the town."

Now the sons of the tsar knew their sister was near. They urged their horses onward toward the castle of gold which stood on a pillar of silver. Above the castle hung a curtain of diamonds, and the stairways, which were made of mother-of-pearl, opened and closed like wings.

At that moment Vasilisa Golden Tress was looking through her window, and she cried out in joy when she saw her brothers. The dragon was away from the palace, and so the princess sent a servant to meet them and to bring them to her.

Vasilisa was cautious, for she was afraid that the dragon might see them. The two princes had barely entered the palace when the silver pillar groaned, the stairways opened, and all the roofs glittered. "The dragon is returning," Vasilisa said. "That is why the castle turns around. Hide quickly, my brothers!"

She had scarcely said this when the dragon flew in, crying in a thunderous voice, "What living man is here?"

"See here, dragon," answered the tsar's sons fearlessly. "We have come to rescue our sister."

"A pity her rescuers are so puny," said the dragon, and he caught one brother with each wing and struck them against each other. Then the castle guards took the dead princes and threw them in a deep pit.

Vasilisa Golden Tress covered herself with tears. For three days she would take neither food nor drink, but on the fourth day she ate and drank, and began planning how she could free herself from the dragon.

"Mighty dragon," said Vasilisa, "great is your power. Is it true that no enemy can defeat you?"

"Not yet," said the dragon. "It was fated at my birth that my conqueror would be named Ivan Goroh, and he would be born from a pea."

The tsaritsa, mother of Vasilisa Golden Tress, grieved because she had no news of her children for so long. One day she went for a walk in her garden. The day was hot and she was thirsty. Now, in that garden was a white marble well from which sweet water sprang. The tsaritsa was eager to drink from the well's golden cup, and with the water she unknowingly swallowed a pea. The pea burst and the tsaritsa became heavy. The pea increased, and grew, and in time the tsaritsa gave birth to a son named Ivan Goroh.

Ivan Goroh grew plump not by the year but by the hour. He was a lively laughing lad, and at ten years he had become a mighty champion. Then he asked his father the tsar and his mother the tsaritsa if he had any brothers and sisters, and he learned how it happened that the whirlwind had carried off his sister, and how his two brothers had gone in search of her and were lost without tidings.

"Father, Mother," begged Ivan Goroh, "let me go too. Give me your blessing to find my brothers and sister."

"What are you saying, my child?" asked the tsar and tsaritsa at once. "You are still young. Your brothers went and were lost. You will be lost too."

"Maybe not," said Ivan Goroh. "I want to find my brothers and sister."

The tsar and tsaritsa pleaded and begged, but Ivan begged and pleaded. So they prepared him for the road, and let him go with tears in their eyes.

Ivan Goroh travelled one day, he travelled another. Toward night he came to a dark forest, and in that forest was a little house on hen's legs, shaking and turning. Ivan spoke the words he had learned in fairy tales, "Little house, turn your back to the forest and your front to me." The cabin turned around to Ivan, and an old Baba Yaga poked her head out the window and asked who he was.

"Grandmother, I am called Ivan Goroh," he answered. "Tell me, have you noticed in what direction the passing whirlwind carries beautiful maidens?"

"Oh, young man," said she. "That whirlwind has frightened me so much that I haven't left my cabin for a hundred and twenty years. That is not a whirlwind, anyway. It is the horse of the dragon."

"Where does he live? I would like to go there," said Ivan.

"What are you thinking of? The dragon would swallow you."

"Maybe not."

"Be sure he doesn't, my champion. But if you should find him, and return this way, promise to bring me some of the water of youth from the dragon's castle," she said, gnashing her teeth fiercely.

"I will get it for you, grandmother. I give you my word."

"I believe you. Now, go straight to where the sun sets, and in one year you will reach the bald mountain. Then ask for directions to the dragon's kingdom."

Then Ivan Goroh went toward the sunset. He passed through three kingdoms and came into the dragon's domain. By the gates of a town he met a beggar—a lame, blind old man with a crutch. Ivan Goroh gave him a silver coin and asked if Vasilisa Golden Tress was in that town.

"Yes, she is, though it is forbidden to say so," answered the beggar.

Ivan then knew that his sister was near. The hero boldly approached the palace. Vasilisa Golden Tress was looking out the window to see if the dragon was returning when from afar she saw Ivan, the young champion, and wished to know who he was. She sent a servant to learn from what land he had come, and what family, and hearing that he was her youngest brother, Vasilisa ran to him and cried, "Run, brother, quickly! The dragon will soon be here, and he will destroy you."

"My dear sister," answered Ivan, "I have no fear of the dragon."

"Are you Ivan Goroh, then?" she asked.

"I am, Sister. Now I will sit down and rest a moment, for I am tired from the road."

Vasilisa commanded that a strong chair be brought, but the chair broke under Ivan and flew into bits. Another chair was brought, all bound with iron, and that one cracked and bent.

"Brother," said Vasilisa, "that was the chair of the dragon."

"Now it is clear that I am heavier than he," laughed Ivan Goroh. He rose and went outside the castle to the forge, and he ordered the dragon's blacksmiths to forge him an iron club nine tons in weight. The blacksmiths hastened to their work. They hammered night and day, and in forty hours the work was done. Fifty men were barely able to carry the club, but Ivan Goroh seized it in one hand and hurled it to the sky. It flew and whirled above the clouds, and vanished from sight. All the people ran in terror thinking that if the club fell on the town, it would crush everyone, and if it fell into the sea, it would raise a tidal wave and drown everyone.

But Ivan Goroh went back to the castle, and gave the command that he be told when the club was coming. They waited an hour, they waited two. After the third hour, the people ran to say that the club was coming. Ivan Goroh caught the club, which bent against his hand. He pressed the club against his knee, straightened it, and went to the castle.

All at once a terrible whistling sound was heard. The dragon was racing homeward. The whirlwind, his horse, flying like an arrow, was breathing fire. Whenever the dragon flew home, the whole castle would quiver and whirl and dance—but not this time. It was clear that someone strong sat inside. The dragon whistled and shouted. The whirlwind, his horse, shook his dark mane, opened his broad wings, reared and roared. The dragon flew right up to the castle, but still the castle did not move.

"Is Ivan Goroh in my house?" the dragon called out. "I'll put him on the palm of one hand, and slap him with the other, and they won't find his bones."

"We shall see about that," said Ivan Goroh.

He went outside, carrying his club. Then the dragon flew up and aimed his spear at Ivan Goroh, but Ivan sprang to one side, and the spear missed.

"Now I'll finish you!" roared Ivan Goroh. He raised his great iron club and struck the dragon a blow that tore him to pieces. The club went across the world, through two kingdoms, and landed in the third.

People hurled up their caps and asked Ivan Goroh to be their tsar. But Ivan brought the blacksmith before them and told the people to follow the smith in doing good. Ivan found the water of life, and sprinkled it on his brothers. They rubbed their eyes. "How long have we slept?" they asked.

"Without me, you would have slept forever, my dear brothers," said Ivan Goroh, pressing them to his heart.

He did not forget to take the dragon's water with him. Ivan made a ship, and on the swan's river they sailed through three kingdoms into the fourth. He did not forget the old Baba Yaga in the cabin. He let her wash in the water, and afterwards she turned into a young woman, and began to sing and dance.

The tsar and tsaritsa met them with joy and honor. They sent word to every land that Vasilisa Golden Tress had returned. A bridegroom came to Vasilisa, and brides were found for her brothers, and weddings were celebrated. On the death of his father, Ivan Goroh became tsar and ruled the land with renown, so that age after age his name has been famous.

The Three Daughters of King O'Hara

[IRELAND]

oluath O'Hara was king long ago in Desmond, and he had three lovely daughters. One time, when the king was away, the eldest one took a thought that she'd like to be married. So she went up in the castle, put on the cloak of darkness her father owned, and wished for the most beautiful man under the sun as a husband. Scarcely had she taken off the cloak when a golden coach came, drawn by four horses, two black and two white, and the finest man she had ever laid eyes on took her away. When the second daughter saw what had happened to her sister, she put on the cloak of darkness and wished for the next best man in the world as a husband. Then a man nearly as marvelous as the first arrived in a golden coach drawn by four black horses and took her away. As for the third sister, she put on the cloak and wished for the best white dog in the world, and soon he came, in a golden coach and four snow white horses, and took the youngest sister away.

When the king arrived home, his stable boy told him what his daughters had done while he was gone. Their father was angry most of all when he heard that his youngest daughter had wished for a white dog, and then gone off with him.

When they got to his place, the husband of the first sister asked, "Would you rather I be a handsome man during the daytime, or a handsome man during the night?" "A handsome man as you are now in the daytime," she replied. And so her husband was a handsome man in the daytime, but at night he was a seal.

The second sister's husband asked her the same question and received the same reply. So her man was a seal at night also.

When the third sister came to the place where the white dog lived, he asked, "Would you like me as I am now in the daytime, or as I am now in the nighttime?" "As you are now in the day," she said. So the white dog was a dog in the daytime, but at night he was the most beautiful of men.

After a time, the youngest sister had a son. And one day when her husband was going out to hunt, he warned her that if anything happened to the child, she should not shed a single tear. While he was away, a great gray crow came and carried the child off. Remembering her husband's warning, the princess did not shed a tear.

All went well until a second son was born. Again her husband said she must not shed a tear if anything happened to the baby. When the child was a week old, a gray crow came and carried him off, but the princess did not let one tear fall.

All went well until a daughter was born, and when she was a week old, a great gray crow came and swept her away. This time the princess dropped one tear onto a handkerchief, and she put the handkerchief in her pocket. When the husband came home from hunting and heard what the crow had done, he asked the princess, "Have you shed tears this time?" "I have dropped one tear," said she. He was angry, for he knew there was harm in that tear.

Then one day King O'Hara invited his three daughters and their husbands to come to a great feast in their honor. The king was very glad to see his children, but the queen was unhappy, for she thought it disgraceful that her youngest daughter had no one to come home with but a white dog.

The white dog was in dread that the king wouldn't let him inside the castle for the feast, but would drive him into the yard, and the other dogs would tear him to pieces. But his wife comforted him. "Wherever I am, you will be," she said, "and wherever you go, I'll follow and take care of you."

When all was ready for the feast at the castle, the king wanted to send the white dog outside to the yard. But the youngest princess refused, and wouldn't let the white dog out of her sight. She kept him by her side during the feast, dividing with him the food that came to herself.

After the feast, when all the guests had left, the three sisters went to their own rooms in the castle. Late in the evening the queen looked into her daughters' rooms as they slept. She went to where the two elder daughters were sleeping and there, instead of the two men who had brought them to the feast, lay two seals, fast asleep. Then she looked into the room of her youngest daughter, and who should she see lying by her side but the most beautiful man she had ever laid eyes on. The white dog's skin lay on the floor, and the queen caught it up and threw it into the kitchen fire. The dog's skin was not five minutes in the flames when it burst with a great crack that woke everyone in the castle, and everyone for miles around as well.

The husband of the youngest princess sprang from the bed, angry and sorry, and said, "If I had been able to spend three nights with you under your father's roof, I would have had my own human form for always and ever, and could have been a man both in the day and the night. But now I must leave you and go away."

He ran out of the castle as fast as his two legs would carry him, but his wife ran after him, and just as fast, and never lost sight of him. He told her to go back to her father, but she wouldn't listen. At nightfall they came to a house, and the man said, "Go inside and stay in this house until morning, and I'll pass the night outside."

The princess went inside, and the woman of the house rose up, gave her a pleasant welcome, and put a good supper before her. Later, a small boy came up to the princess' knee and called her "Mother." The woman of the house told the child to go back to his room, and she warned him not to come out again.

"Here are a pair of scissors," said the woman of the house to the king's daughter, "and they will serve you well. Whatever ragged people you see, if you cut a piece off their rags, their clothes will turn to gold."

Next morning the princess went out, and her husband said, "You'd better go home now to your father." "I'll not go to my father if I have to leave you," said she. So he went on and she followed. It was that way all the day till night came, and at nightfall they saw another house at the foot of a hill. Again her husband said, "You go inside, and I'll stay outside till morning."

The woman of the house made her welcome. After the princess had something to eat and drink, a little boy came out of another room, ran to her knee, and called her "Mother." The woman of the house sent the boy back to where he had come from, and told him to stay there.

Next morning, when the princess was leaving, the woman of the house gave her a comb and said, "If you meet any person who has a head that is sore and scabby, just draw this comb over it three times, and their head will be cured, and covered with beautiful golden hair as well."

The princess took the comb and went out to her husband. "Leave me now," he said. "Go back to your own father." "I will not," said she. On they traveled, and at nightfall they came to a third house at the foot of a hill where the princess received a good welcome. After she had eaten, a little girl with only one eye came to her knee and called her "Mother."

The princess began to cry at the sight of this child, thinking that she herself was the cause that it had but one eye. She put her hand into her pocket where she kept the handkerchief on which she had dropped the tear when the gray crow took her baby away. She had not dared use the handkerchief since that day, for an eye appeared on it. The princess opened the handkerchief and put the eye in the girl's head, where it grew at once, and the child saw out of it as well as out of the other eye. Then the woman of the house sent the girl to bed.

Next morning, when the princess was leaving, the woman gave her a whistle and said, "Whenever you put this whistle to your mouth and blow on it, all the birds of the air will come to you from every quarter under the sun. Take care of the whistle, for it will serve you well in the hour of your greatest need."

"Go back to your father's castle," her husband said when she came to him. "The Queen of Tir na n-Og, the Land of Youth, has me under an enchantment, and today I must go to her underground kingdom and be her husband."

He got up, and went a few steps forward to some bulrushes, pulled up one, and disappeared into the hole where the rush had been.

The princess sat lamenting on the mound until evening, but at last she came to her senses. Going over to the rushes, she pulled up a stalk and went into the earth, and followed her husband until she came to the lower world.

She walked until she saw a splendid castle, and nearby was a small house. She went to the house and asked if she could stay until morning, and the woman of the house welcomed her.

The next day, the woman was washing clothes, for that was how she made a living. The princess was helping the washerwoman with her work, and she learned that it was the wedding day of the Queen of Tir na n-Og. She guessed who the queen's husband would be.

Not far from the washerwoman, there lived a henwife and her two ragged little daughters. One of them came to the washerwoman's house to play, and the princess saw that the child's clothes were torn and dirty. So she took her scissors and cut the girl's ragged dress, and at once it became the most beautiful dress that was ever seen in that kingdom.

When she saw what happened to her dress, the child ran home to her mother as fast as she could. "Who gave you that dress?" her mother asked. "The stranger that stays with the washerwoman," answered the little girl.

News of the magic scissors soon reached the Queen of Tir na n-Og, who sent a messenger to the washerwoman's house to fetch them. The princess sent word back that she would give the scissors to the queen if she could pass one night with the queen's husband. The queen answered that she was willing, and then she gave her husband a potion that made him fall into a deep sleep till morning.

The next day, the henwife's second daughter came to play, and she was a wretched little thing, and her head was covered with scabs and sores. The princess took out her comb and drew it three times over the child's head. The little girl ran home and told her mother how the stranger had used a comb to cure her, and give her golden hair.

Word of the magic comb soon reached the queen, who sent messengers to the washerwoman's house demanding to have it. The princess answered that she would give up the comb if she might again pass one night with the queen's husband. The queen agreed, and again she gave her husband a sleeping potion so that when the princess came he was fast asleep and did not awaken until after she had left the next morning.

On the third day, the princess went for a walk with the henwife's two daughters, and when they were outside the town, she took the whistle and put it to her mouth and blew. Birds flew to her from every direction in great flocks, and among the rest was a bird of song and new tales. The princess took this bird on her shoulder and told it about her terrible trouble.

"The queen has been giving your husband a sleeping potion each time you go to his chamber. Tonight you must get word to his servant not to let him drink it," the bird told her.

"And how can I break the queen's power over him?" asked the princess.

"The only person in Tir na n-Og who can do that is her husband," said the bird. "Her power lies inside the holly tree that grows in front of the castle. Inside the tree is a sheep, inside the sheep is a duck, inside the duck is an egg, and inside the egg is her power and her life. Only the queen's husband can cut down the holly tree."

When the henwife's daughters went home, they told their mother about the whistle, and news of the whistle soon reached the queen, who sent for the whistle at once. The princess answered that she would exchange this treasure for one night with the queen's husband. But she made sure also to send a message to her husband's servant, as the bird had told her.

When the princess arrived at the castle, she found her husband awake, and she told him about the holly tree, the sheep, the duck, and the egg that held the queen's life. The husband then took an axe and went to the holly tree. He struck it a few blows, and it split open, releasing the sheep. He grabbed the sheep, and out flew the duck, he squeezed the duck, and the egg dropped out and smashed against the ground, and that was the end of the Queen of Tir na n-Og.

Then the husband embraced his true wife, and they held a great feast. The two of them have never left Tir na n-Og, and as they are now living happily there, so may we live happily here.

Three Golden Hairs
of Grandfather Allknow

[CZECH REPUBLIC]

nce upon a time there was a king who loved nothing more than to hunt wild animals. One day he chased a stag deep into the woods, and found himself lost and alone as night descended. He saw a light in the distance, and followed it until he came to the cottage of a poor woodcutter. The king asked the man to guide him back to the main road, promising to pay him well in return. "I would gladly do so," said the woodcutter, "but my wife is about to have a baby, and I cannot leave her. Please stay with us tonight, and I will make a bed for you in the loft. Tomorrow I will guide you out of the forest." A baby boy was born that night in the small cottage, and as the mother and father slept, the king looked down and saw a light in the room below. Three strange old women, all dressed in white, stood over the baby, and each one held a lighted candle in her hand.

The first woman said, "My gift to this boy is that he shall come into great dangers." The second said, "My gift to him is that he shall escape from all the dangers, and live a long life." And the third said, "My gift to him is that he shall marry the baby daughter who has been born this day to the wife of the king who lies upstairs in the loft." Then the three women put out their candles, and all was dark and quiet again. Those three strange women were the Fates.

The king felt as if a sword had been thrust into his heart. He vowed that he would do anything to keep this boy from marrying his daughter.

At dawn, the baby began to cry. The woodcutter arose and discovered that his wife was dead.

"Oh, my poor little motherless child," he cried. "What will become of you?"

"Give the baby to me," said the king. "I will make sure that he is well cared for, and I will give you so much money that you will never need to chop wood again as long as you live."

The woodcutter was delighted to accept this offer, and the king promised to send for the baby later. When he arrived at the palace he learned that a beautiful baby daughter had indeed been born to him the day before. He called one of his servants and ordered him to go to the woodcutter's cottage and to give the man a bag of gold in exchange for his baby.

"Drown the child on your way back," the king told him. "If you don't drown it, you shall drink water yourself."

The servant went to the woodcutter's cottage,

and got the baby, and put it into a basket. When he came to a bridge across a deep and broad river, he set the basket into the water, and it floated away.

"Good bye, uninvited son-in-law," said the king, when the servant told him what he had done.

The king thought the baby was drowned, but it wasn't. The boy floated along in the basket quite happily, and slept as if the river were singing to him, until a fisherman saw the basket and drew him ashore. He carried the baby to his wife and said, "You have always wanted a little son, and now the river has brought us one." They raised the boy as their own, and called him Floatling, because he had floated to them on the river.

The river flowed on, years passed, and the baby became a boy, and the boy became a handsome youth. One day in the summer it came to pass that the king rode that way all alone. He was hot and thirsty, and he asked the fisherman for a drink of fresh water. It was Floatling who brought the water to him. The king was surprised to find such a strong and handsome young man in a fisherman's hut. "Is he your son?" the king asked.

"Yes and no," answered the fisherman. "Just twenty years ago a little baby floated down the river to us in a basket, and we have brought him up." A mist came before the king's eyes, and he turned pale, for he knew that this was the boy he had ordered to be drowned. But he soon regained control of himself. He sprang down from his horse and said, "I need a messenger to go at once to the palace. Can this young man go there for me?"

"Your majesty has only to command and the

lad will go," the fisherman answered. The king sat down and wrote a letter to the queen—

> *The man who carries this message is a dangerous enemy of mine. Put him to death immediately. Let it be done before my return.*

Floatling set out at once carrying the letter, but his path led through a great dark forest, and he lost his way. At length he met an old woman who asked, "Where are you going, Floatling?"

"I am carrying a letter to the king's palace, and have lost my way. Can you tell me how to find the road?"

"You won't find it tonight," she said. "Stay the night with me, please. You won't be a stranger, for I am your godmother."

The young man agreed, and they hadn't gone far when a little house appeared before them, just as if it had grown all at once out of the ground. During the night, as the lad slept, the woman took the letter out of his pocket and put another in its place, on which was written—

> *I have chosen this young man to be my son-in-law. Have him married to our daughter at once. Let it be done before my return.*

After the queen had read the letter, she made arrangements at once for the wedding, for both she and the princess were charmed by Floatling. And he was just as pleased with his royal bride. Some days later the king returned home, and when he learned what had happened, he flew into a rage.

"But you yourself ordered me to have him married to our daughter before you returned," said the queen, and she showed him the letter. The handwriting, seal, and paper were indeed his own. The king then summoned the woodcutter's son. "What is done cannot be undone," the king told him. "But a king's daughter is not earned so easily, and you may not live here as her husband until you bring me three golden hairs from the head of Grandfather Allknow."

Floatling said goodbye to his bride and went forth, and since his godmother was one of the three Fates, it was easy for him to find the right road. He went far and wide, over hill and dale, until he came to the Black Sea, where he saw a boat, and in it stood a ferryman.

"God bless you, old ferryman," said Floatling.

"God grant it, young pilgrim. Where are you traveling?"

"To Grandfather Allknow, to get three of his golden hairs."

"I have long been waiting for a messenger such as you," said the ferryman. "For twenty years I have been ferrying without rest, and no one has come to relieve me. If you promise to ask Grandfather Allknow when my labors will end, I will ferry you across the Black Sea."

Floatling gave his word, and the ferryman took him across. Soon he came to a great city that was fallen into ruin, and he met an old man who leaned on a staff and could barely stand.

"God bless you, grandfather," Floatling said.

"God grant it, handsome youth. Where are you going?"

"To ask Grandfather Allknow for three of his golden hairs."

"Ah! We have long been waiting for such a messenger. I must take you at once to our king."

When they arrived at the palace, the king said, "I hear that you are going on an errand to Grandfather Allknow. In this city, we once had a tree which bore the apples of youth, and even if a person were on the brink of death, he had only to take one bite to become young again. But for the last twenty years our apple tree has produced no fruit. If you promise to ask Grandfather Allknow how we can revive our tree, I will reward you well."

Floatling gave his word, and he traveled until he came to another great city that lay in ruin. Near the city, a young man was burying his father, and tears rolled down his cheeks as he worked.

"God bless you, mournful grave digger," said Floatling.

"God grant it, traveler. Where are you going?"

"I am going to Grandfather Allknow to ask for three of his golden hairs."

"To Grandfather Allknow? It's a pity you did not come sooner! Our king has long been waiting for such a messenger. I must take you to him"

When they got there, the king said, "I hear that you are going on an errand to Grandfather Allknow. In this city, we once had a fountain, and out of this fountain flowed the water of life. If a person drank it, even if he were on the brink of death, he would recover at once. And if a person were already dead, and this water were sprinkled upon him, he would immediately rise up and walk. But for the past twenty years, the water has ceased to flow. If you promise to ask Grandfather Allknow how we may restore our fountain, I will give you a great reward."

Floatling promised, and the king dismissed him graciously. After this, he traveled through a dark forest, and in the midst of that forest he came to a wide green meadow full of beautiful flowers, and in the meadow stood the golden palace of Grandfather Allknow, and it glittered as if on fire. Floatling went inside the palace and there he found an old woman sitting and spinning in a corner.

"Welcome, Floatling. I am delighted to see you again," she said. It was none other than his godmother, at whose house he had spent the night when he was carrying the letter. "What has brought you here?' she asked.

"The king refuses to accept me as his son-in-law until I bring him three golden hairs from Grandfather Allknow."

The old woman smiled and said, "Grandfather Allknow is the bright sun, and I am his mother. In the morning, he is a little boy, at noon a grown man, and in the evening an old grandfather. I will provide you with the three golden hairs from his head, so that I may not be your godmother for nothing. But, my boy, you must not let him see you. My son is certainly a good soul, but when he comes home hungry in the evening, it might easily happen that he would roast you and eat you for his supper. Hide under that empty tub over there."

Floatling begged her also to ask Grandfather Allknow about the ferryman, the apple tree, and the fountain. "I will," she promised.

All at once a wind arose and in flew the sun, an old grandfather with a golden head. "A smell, a smell of human flesh!" cried he. "Are you hiding someone here, Mother?"

"How could I hide anyone from you?" she asked. The old man said nothing but sat down to his supper, and afterwards he laid his head on the old woman's lap and fell asleep. As soon as she saw that he was sound asleep, she pulled out a hair and threw it on the ground, where it rang like a harp string.

"What is it?" asked Grandfather Allknow.

"I was asleep," said the old woman, "and I had a strange dream. I dreamed of a city where the water of life flowed from a fountain. But for the last twenty years the fountain has been dry. Is there any way it may be made to flow again?"

"That is quite easy," he replied. "There is a toad sitting under the fountain that won't let the water flow. Let them clean out the well, and kill the toad, and the water will flow as before."

When the old man fell asleep again, the old woman pulled out a second golden hair and threw it on the ground.

"What ails you, Mother?"

"I was asleep, and again had a strange dream. I dreamed of a city where a tree bore the apples of youth. When anyone grew old, he had only to take one bite to become young again. But for the last twenty years the tree has borne no fruit. Is there any hope for those people?"

"Yes, to be sure. Under the tree there lies a snake which robs it of its magical powers. Let them kill the snake and transplant the apple tree. Then it will bear fruit as before."

The old man fell asleep again, and then the old woman pulled out a third golden hair.

"Why won't you let me rest, Mother?" cried Grandfather Allknow.

"I didn't want to wake you, but a heavy sleep fell upon me, and I had another strange dream. For twenty years, a ferryman has been rowing on the Black Sea, and no one has come to take his place. When will his work end?"

"He only needs to put the oar into another person's hand and jump ashore, and that person will become ferryman," said Grandfather Allknow. "Now let me sleep in peace. Tomorrow I must arise early, and go dry the tears the king's daughter sheds every night for her husband, the woodcutter's son, whom the king has sent for three of my golden hairs."

In the morning a wind again arose outside, and a beautiful golden-haired child awoke on the old woman's lap. The sun said farewell to his mother and flew out by the east window. Then the old woman went to the tub and said to Floatling, "Here are the three golden hairs for you, and I trust that you heard the answers to your questions. Go now. You will not see me again."

Floatling thanked his godmother and went on

his way. When he came to the first city, the king asked him what news he brought.

"Good news," said Floatling. "Clean out the fountain and kill the toad that sits there. Then the water of life will flow again as in the old days." The king did this, and when he saw the water of life bubbling up, he gave Floatling twelve horses as white as swans, laden with gold and silver.

When Floatling came to the second city, the king asked him what news he brought.

"Good news," was the reply. "Have the apple tree dug up, and you will find a snake under the roots. Kill it, then plant the tree again, and it will bear fruit as before." They did this at once, and the next day the tree was covered with flowers. The king was delighted. He presented Floatling with twelve horses as black as ravens, and on them as much riches as they could carry.

Floatling traveled on, and when he came to the Black Sea, the ferryman asked him whether he had learned how he could free himself.

"I have," said Floatling. "But I can only tell you after you ferry me across." At first the man refused, but when he saw that there was no other way to know the answer, he ferried Floatling and his horses across the water.

"Listen well," Floatling said. "When you ferry the next person across, put the oar into that person's hand and jump ashore. You will be free, and he will become ferryman in your place."

The king could scarcely believe his eyes when Floatling gave him the three golden hairs, and the princess wept tears of joy at her husband's return.

"Where did you get these beautiful horses and this great wealth?" the king asked.

"I earned them," said Floatling, and he told how he had helped one king regain the apples of youth which made old people young again, and how he had helped another king restore the water of life which makes sick people well and returns the dead to life.

"Apples of youth! Water of life!" cried the king. "I could become young again and never die!" He started off down the road that Floatling had taken without even saying goodbye. But he hasn't returned yet. Some people report that he has been seen rowing travelers across the Black Sea. Thus did Floatling, the woodcutter's son, become king of that country, as the Fates had once predicted.

Twelve Wild Ducks

[NORWAY]

nce upon a time there was a queen, and she went out riding one day in her sleigh on the new-fallen snow. And when she had gone a little way, she began to bleed at the nose, and had to get out of the sleigh. As she stood there, leaning against a fence, and looked upon the red blood on the white snow, she fell to thinking how she had twelve sons and no daughter, and she said to herself, "If only I had a daughter, as white as snow and as red as blood, I shouldn't care at all what became of my sons." These words were scarcely out of her mouth when an old witch of the trolls came up to her. "A daughter you shall have," said the troll, "and she shall be as white as snow and as red as blood, and your sons shall be mine, though you may keep them till the babe is christened. So when the time came, the queen had a daughter, and she was as white as snow and as red as blood, just as the troll had promised, and they named her Snow-White-and-Rosy-Red.

Well, there was great joy at the king's court, and the queen was glad as glad could be. But when what she had promised the old witch came to her mind, she sent for the silversmith and bade him make twelve silver spoons, one for each prince, and after that she bade him make one more, and that she gave to Snow-White-and-Rosy-Red. And as soon as the princess was christened, the princes turned into twelve wild ducks and flew away.

The princess grew up, and she was both tall and fair. But she was often sad and no one could understand why. One evening, her mother asked her, "Why are you so sorrowful, my daughter? Is there anything you want? If so, only say the word and you shall have it."

"Oh, I am so lonely here," said Snow-White-and-Rosy-Red. "Everyone else has brothers and sisters, but I am all alone, and that is why I am so sorrowful."

"But you did have brothers," said the queen. "I had twelve sons who were your brothers, but I gave them all away to get you." And she told the girl the whole story.

Afterwards, the princess had no peace, for in spite of all the queen could say or do, she wanted to set out and seek her brothers, and at last she was given leave to do so. She walked on and on, farther than you would imagine a young maiden would have strength to go.

One day, when she was walking through a great wood, she felt tired and sat down on a mossy tuft and fell asleep. She dreamed that she went deeper and deeper into the wood until she came to a tiny wooden hut, and that she found her brothers there. She awoke, and right in front of her was a worn path in the green moss, and this path led deeper into the wood. She followed it, and after a long time she came to a little wooden house just like the one she had seen in her dream. When she went inside, there was no one at home. She looked around and saw twelve beds, and twelve chairs, and twelve spoons—a dozen of everything.

Snow-White-and-Rosy-Red guessed at once that her brothers lived here, and she was happier than she had been in many years. She kindled a fire, and swept the room, and made the beds, and cooked dinner, and made the house as tidy as she could, and when she had done all this work, she ate her own dinner and crept under the bed of her youngest brother. But she left her own silver spoon on the table.

She had scarcely gotten down under the bed when she heard something flapping and whirring in the air, and twelve wild ducks came sweeping in, and as soon as they entered the house they became princes.

"How nice and warm it is here," they said. "May heaven bless the person who made the fire and cooked such a good dinner for us."

And so each of the princes took up his silver spoon, and was about to eat, when they noticed that there was one more spoon lying on the table, and it was so like the others that they couldn't tell it from theirs.

"This is our sister's spoon," they said, "and if her spoon is here, she can't be very far off herself."

"If this is our sister's spoon, and she is here," said the eldest, "she should die, for she is to blame for all our suffering."

"No," said the youngest, "it would be wrong to hurt her. If there is anyone to blame, it is our own mother."

They searched high and low for their sister, and looked for her under all the beds, and when they came to the youngest prince's bed, they found her and dragged her out. Then the eldest prince wished again to have her killed.

"Oh, please, don't kill me!" she cried. "I've been seeking you for three years, and if I could only release you from your enchantment, I would willingly give my own life."

"Well," said they, "there is a way that you can set us free, if you choose to do so."

"Yes, tell me!" cried the princess.

"You must pick thistledown," said the princes, "and you must card it, and spin it, and weave it. And after you've done that, you must cut out and make twelve coats, twelve shirts, and twelve neckerchiefs, one for each of us, and while you are doing all this, you must neither talk, nor laugh, nor weep. If you can do this, we are free."

"But where shall I find enough thistledown for so many neckerchiefs and shirts and coats?" asked Snow-White-and-Rosy-Red.

"We'll show you," said the princes, and they led her to a great wide meadow where there grew thousands of thistles, all nodding in the breeze, the down floating and shimmering in the air. The princess had never seen so much thistledown in her life, and she set to work at once to gather it. When she got home that night to the little house, she began carding and spinning yarn from the down. She worked long and hard. Each day she cleaned the house and cooked dinner for her brothers, who came flying home in the evening as wild ducks, and were princes at night. In the morning, they would fly off again, and were wild ducks the whole day.

Now it happened once, when the maiden was in the meadow gathering thistledown, that the king who ruled that land was out hunting, and he saw Snow-White-and-Rosy-Red. He wondered who she was, and he stopped and asked her name, but she did not answer. He took her up onto his horse, and then she made signs to the king, and pointed to the bags that held her work, and so the king told his men to bring the bags with them.

The king was a wise and handsome man, and gentle and kind to Snow-White-and-Rosy-Red, but the old queen, who was the king's stepmother, was jealous of her, and said that the maiden must surely be a witch—otherwise, why didn't she talk, or laugh, or weep?

But the king wouldn't listen to her, and he married Snow-White-and-Rosy-Red, and they lived together happily. And she kept sewing her shirts.

When nearly a year had passed, Snow-White-and-Rosy-Red brought a little prince into the world. Then the old queen was even more spiteful and jealous, and so in the dead of night she took away the little baby, and threw it into a pit full of snakes. Afterwards she cut Snow-White-and-Rosy-Red on her finger, and smeared the blood over her mouth, and went straight to the king, saying, "Now come and see what sort of a creature you have taken for your queen. She has eaten her own baby." The king believed his stepmother. Still, he could not bring himself to punish his wife.

The next year, Snow-White-and-Rosy-Red had another son, and the same thing happened again. The old queen stole the baby while the young queen slept, and she threw it into a pit of snakes, and cut the mother's finger, and smeared the blood over her mouth. She went and told the king that his wife had eaten her own child. The king was so sorrowful, but still he would not punish his wife.

Before the next year was over, Snow-White-and-Rosy-Red brought a daughter into the world, and the old queen took this child, too, and threw her into the pit full of snakes while the young queen slept. Then she cut her finger, smeared the blood over her mouth, and went again to the king and said, "Now you come and see if your wife is not a horrible, wicked witch, for she has gone and eaten up her third babe too."

Then the king was so sad that there was no end to it, and he ordered that she be burned alive on a pile of wood. But just when the pile was set ablaze, and Snow-White-and-Rosy-Red was to be put on it, she took out twelve neckerchiefs, and twelve shirts, and twelve coats, and laid them on twelve boards that were around the pile. As soon as she had done so, down from the sky flew twelve wild ducks. Each one snapped up his clothes in his bill and flew off. But the youngest brother's shirt was unfinished, and lacked a left sleeve.

"Wasn't I right when I told you she was a witch?" said the old queen to the king. "Hurry and burn her while the fire is hot."

"We have plenty of wood," said the king, "and I have a mind to see what will happen next."

Then twelve princes came riding up, and the youngest of them had a duck's wing for one arm. They demanded to know what was happening.

"My queen is about to be burned," said the king. "She is a witch, and has eaten her own babes."

"Speak, sister," the princes said. "You have set us free. Now save yourself."

Snow-White-and-Rosy-Red told how the queen had stolen into her room and taken her babes away, and cut her little finger and smeared the blood over her mouth. Then the princes took the king and showed him the snake pit where the three babes lay playing with adders and toads, and lovelier children you never saw.

So the king had the babes taken out of the snake pit at once. He ordered that the old queen be bound fast between twelve unbroken horses. Then the king took Snow-White-and-Rosy-Red and their three children, and the twelve princes, and they all went to the young queen's father and mother, and there was joy and gladness in the whole kingdom because the princess was saved, and because she had set free her twelve brothers.

How Ian Direach Got the Blue Falcon

[SCOTLAND]

king and queen once ruled over the islands of the west, and they had one son, Ian Direach, whom they loved dearly. The prince grew up to be tall and strong and handsome, and he could run and ride and swim and dive better than any lad of his own age in the entire country. He was skilled at singing and telling stories, and he had a magic harp that played by itself. On long winter evenings when everyone would gather in the great hall to work at shaping bows or weaving cloth, Ian would tell them tales of the deeds of the great heroes, who were his ancestors.

So the time passed until Ian had almost grown to be a man, and then his mother the queen died. There was mourning for her throughout the isles, and the boy and his father mourned her most bitterly of all. But before the new year came, the king married another wife, and seemed to have forgotten the old one. Only Ian remembered.

On a morning when the leaves were yellow on the trees of the glen, Ian slung his bow over his shoulder, filled his quiver with arrows, and went to the hills in search of game. But not a bird was to be seen anywhere, until at length a blue falcon flew past him. He raised his bow and took aim at her. His eye was good and his hand was steady, but the falcon's flight was swift, and his arrow only grazed a feather on her wing. As the sun was now low over the sea, he put the feather in his game bag and set out homewards.

"Have you brought us much game today?" asked his stepmother as he entered the hall.

"Only this," he answered, and he handed her the feather of the blue falcon. She took it by the tip and gazed at it silently. Then she turned to Ian and said, "I am setting upon you this spell, that you may always be cold, and wet, and dirty, that your shoes may ever have water in them, until you bring me the blue falcon on which this feather grew."

"If it is spells you are laying, I can lay them too," answered Ian Direach, "and you shall stand with one foot on the great house and another on the castle until I come back again, and your face shall be to the wind, from wheresoever it blows."

Then Ian Direach went away to seek the bird, as his stepmother bade him. Looking homewards, he saw the queen standing with one foot on the great house and the other on the castle, and her face turned towards whatever tempest should blow.

On he journeyed, over hills and across rivers until he reached a wide plain, but never did he catch a glimpse of the blue falcon. It grew darker, and the small birds were seeking their nests, and at length Ian could see no more, and he lay down under some bushes and sleep came to him. And in his dream a soft nose touched him, and a warm body curled up beside him, and a low voice whispered in his ear, "Fortune is against you, Ian Direach. I have but the cheek and hoof of a sheep to give you, and with these you must be content."

Ian Direach awoke and beheld Martin the fox. Between them they kindled a fire and ate their supper. Then Martin the fox told Ian Direach to lie down as before, and to sleep until morning. And in the morning when he awoke, Martin said, "The falcon that you seek is in the keeping of the Giant of the Five Heads, and the Five Necks, and the Five Humps. I will show you the way to his house, and I advise you to do his bidding nimbly and cheerfully, and above all to treat his birds kindly, for he may give you his falcon to feed and care for. And when this happens, wait till the giant is out of his house, then throw a cloth over the falcon and bear her away with you. Only be sure that not one of her feathers touches anything within the house, or evil will befall you."

"Thank you for your advice," Ian said. "I will be careful to follow it." Then he took the path to the giant's house.

"Who is there?" cried the giant, as someone knocked loudly on the door of his house.

"One who seeks work as a servant," answered Ian Direach.

"And what can you do?" asked the giant.

"I can care for birds and tend pigs. I can feed

and milk a cow, as well as goats and sheep, if you have any of these," replied Ian Direach.

"Then enter, for I have great need of you," said the giant.

So Ian Direach was hired, and he tended all the birds and beasts so well and so carefully that the giant was well pleased and thought that he might even trust the lad to feed the blue falcon. Ian was glad in his heart, and he took such good care of the falcon that her feathers shone like the sky.

One day the giant said to him, "My brothers on the other side of the mountain have been asking me to visit them for a long time, but I could never go for fear of leaving my falcon. Now I think I can trust her with you for one day. I shall be back by nightfall."

Scarcely was the giant out of sight the next morning than Ian Direach seized the falcon, threw a cloth over her head, and carried her toward the door. But the rays of the sun pierced the thickness of the cloth, and as Ian passed through the doorway the bird started. One of its feathers touched the wood post, which gave a scream that brought the giant back home in three strides. Ian Direach trembled for his life, but the giant only said, "If you want my falcon, you must bring me the White Sword of Light that is in the house of the Big Women of Dhiurradh."

"And where do they live?" asked Ian.

"That is for you to discover," said the giant, and Ian dared say no more. He hastened to the river and there, as he hoped, he met his friend Martin the fox, who bade him eat his supper and lie down to sleep. The next morning, the fox said, "Let us go down to the shore of the sea." And to the shore of the sea they went, and beheld the water stretching before them, and the isle of Dhiurradh in the midst of it. Ian Direach's heart sank, and he turned to Martin the fox and asked why he had brought him there, for without a boat he could never find the Big Women.

"Do not despair," answered the fox, "for I will change myself into a boat, and you shall go on board me, and I will carry you over the sea to the Seven Big Women of Dhiurradh. Tell them that you are skilled in the brightening of silver and gold, and in the end they will take you as a servant. If you please them, they will give you the White Sword of Light to make bright and shining. But when you seek to steal it, take good care that its sheath touches nothing inside the house, or evil will befall you."

Ian Direach did all things as the fox told him, and the Seven Big Women of Dhiurradh took him for their servant, and for six weeks he worked so hard that his seven mistresses said to each other, "Never has a servant had the skill to make everything so bright and shining as this one does. Let us give him the White Sword of Light to polish like the rest."

Then they brought forth the White Sword of Light from the iron closet where it hung, and bade him rub it till he could see his face in the shining blade, and he did so. Then one day, when the Seven Big Women were away, he decided that the moment had come for him to carry off the sword.

Placing it in its sheath, he hoisted it to his shoulder. But just as he was passing through the door, the tip of the sheath touched the wood, and the door gave a loud shriek. The Big Women heard it and came running back and took the sword from him, saying, "If it is our sword you want, you must first bring us the bay colt of the King of Ireland."

Humbled and ashamed, Ian left the house. He sat down by the side of the sea, and soon Martin the fox came to him.

"I can see that you have taken no heed of my warning, Ian Direach," said Martin the fox. "But have some food, and I will help you once again."

At these words Ian Direach regained his courage. He gathered sticks and made a fire and ate with Martin the fox. He slept there on the sand, and at dawn the next morning Martin said to Ian Direach, "I will change myself into a ship, and will carry you across the seas to Ireland. You shall offer to serve in the king's stables and tend his horses until he is so pleased with you that he gives you the bay colt to wash and brush. But when you run away with her, be sure that only the soles of her hooves touch anything within the palace gates, or it will go badly for you."

After he had given this advice to Ian Direach, the fox changed himself into a ship, and set sail for Ireland. And the king of that country gave into Ian Direach's hands the care of his horses. Never before had their coats shone so brightly, nor was their pace so swift, and the king was well pleased. At the end of a month he sent for Ian and said to him, "You have given me faithful service, and now I will entrust you with the most precious thing that my kingdom holds." He led Ian Direach to the stable where the bay colt stood. Ian groomed her and fed her and galloped with her all around the country until he could outrun the wind that was behind him and overtake the wind in front.

"I am going away to hunt," said the king one morning while he was watching Ian tend the bay colt in her stable. The king left, and when he was no longer in sight, Ian Direach led the bay colt out of the stable, and sprang on her back. But as they rode through the gate which stood between the palace and the outer world, the colt swished her tail against the post, which shrieked loudly. In a moment the king came running up and seized the colt's bridle.

"If you want my bay colt, you must first bring me the daughter of the King of France," said the King of Ireland.

With slow steps Ian Direach walked down to the shore where Martin the fox awaited him.

"Plainly I see that you have not done as I bid you, nor will you ever do it," said the fox. "But I will help you again. For a third time I will change myself into a ship, and we will sail to France."

And to France they sailed, and as he was the ship, Martin the fox sailed wherever he wished, and ran himself into the cleft of a rock high on the land. He told Ian Direach to go up to the king's palace and say that he had been shipwrecked. Ian Direach listened to the words of the fox, and he told a tale so pitiful that the king and queen, and the princess their daughter, all came out to hear it.

And when they had heard it, they wanted to go to the shore and visit the ship which now was floating, for the tide was up. Torn and battered was the ship, as if it had passed through many dangers, yet music of a wondrous sweetness poured forth from within.

"Bring your ship closer," cried the princess, "so that I may go and see for myself the harp that plays so sweetly."

A rowboat was brought, and Ian Direach and the princess stepped inside and rowed to the larger vessel. Ian helped the princess aboard, and they went in search of the source of the music, which always sounded sweeter, yet they could never find its source. When at last they reached the deck, no land was in sight, and the ship was racing across the water.

The princess stood silent. "An evil trick have you played on me! Where are we going?"

"To make you a queen," said Ian Direach, "for the king of Ireland sent me to find you, and in return he will give me his bay colt, and I will take the bay colt to the Seven Big Women of Dhiurradh, and they will give me the White Sword of Light. I must carry the Sword of Light to the Giant of the Five Heads and Five Necks and Five Humps, and he will give me the blue falcon which I have promised my stepmother so that she will free me from the spell which she has laid on me."

"Ah, but I would rather marry you," thought the princess.

By and by the ship sailed into a harbor on the coast of Ireland and cast anchor there. Martin the fox told Ian Direach to ask the princess to wait in a cave while they conducted their business on land, and they would return for her as soon as they could. As they touched land, Martin changed himself into a beautiful woman. "Won't I make a fine wife for the king?" he laughed.

Now the King of Ireland had been hunting on the hill, and when he saw a strange ship sailing towards the harbor, he guessed that it might be Ian Direach, and left his hunting and ran down the hill to the stable. Hastily he led the bay colt from its stall and put the golden saddle on her back, and the silver bridle over her head, and hurried to meet the princess.

"I have brought you the King of France's daughter," said Ian Direach. The King of Ireland looked at the maiden, and was pleased. He bowed low and asked her to do him the honor to enter the palace, and as he went in, the fox looked back at Ian Direach and smiled.

In the great hall the king paused and pointed to an iron chest which stood in a corner. "In that chest is the crown that has waited for you for many years," he said, "and at last you have come for it." And he stooped down to unlock the box.

In an instant, Martin the fox sprang onto the king's back and gave him such a bite that he fell down unconscious. Quickly Martin took his own shape and trotted away to the seashore where Ian Direach and the princess and the bay colt awaited him. "I will become a ship," cried Martin the fox, "and you shall go on board me." They set sail and soon they saw the rocks of Dhiurradh before them.

"Let the bay colt and the princess hide in these rocks," said Martin, "and I will change myself into a colt and go with you to the house of the Seven Big Women."

Joy filled the hearts of the Big Women when they beheld Ian leading the bay colt up to their door, and the youngest of them fetched the White Sword of Light, and gave it into the hands of Ian Direach, who took off the golden saddle and the silver bridle and went down the hill with the sword to the place where the princess and the real colt awaited him.

"Now we shall have the ride that we have longed for!" cried the Seven Big Women, and they saddled and bridled the colt. The eldest sister sat in the saddle, and the second sister sat on the back of the first, and the third on the back of the second, and so on for the whole seven. And when they were all seated the eldest struck the colt with a whip, and the beast bounded forward. Over the moors it flew, round and round the mountains, and still the Big Women clung to it and snorted with pleasure. At last it leapt high into the air and came down on top of Monadh, the high hill, where the crag is. And it rested its forelegs on the crag and threw up its hind legs, and the Seven Big Women fell over the crag and landed one on top of the other. And the colt laughed, and became a fox again, and galloped away to the seashore where Ian Direach and the princess and the real colt and the White Sword of Light were awaiting him.

"I will make myself into a ship," said Martin the fox, "and will carry you, and the princess, and the bay colt, and the White Sword of Light back to the land."

When they reached the shore, Martin took his own shape and told Ian Direach, "Let the princess and the bay colt remain here among the rocks with the White Sword of Light, and I will change myself into a likeness of the White Sword of Light, and you shall carry me to to the giant."

From afar, the Giant of the Five Heads and Five Necks and Five Humps beheld the blaze of the White Sword of Light, and his heart rejoiced. He took the blue falcon and put it in a basket and gave it to Ian Direach, who bore it swiftly away to the place where the princess, and the bay colt, and the true Sword of Light awaited.

So delighted was the giant to possess the sword he had coveted for many a year that he began at once to whirl it through the air, and to cut and slash with it. For a little while, Martin let the giant play with him. Then he twisted a bit in the giant's hand, and cut through the five necks, so that five heads rolled upon the floor. Then he ran back to Ian Direach and said, "Saddle the colt with the golden saddle, and bridle it with the silver bridle, and sling the basket with the falcon over your shoulders, and hold the White Sword of Light with its back against your nose. Then mount the colt, and let the princess mount behind you, and ride to your father's palace. But be sure that the back of the sword is always against your nose, or else when your stepmother sees you she will change you into a dry twig. If you do as I bid you, however, she herself will become a bundle of sticks."

Ian Direach followed Martin the fox's advice faithfully. His stepmother fell as a bundle of sticks before him, and the fate she had planned for him fell upon herself. Ian Direach promised Martin the fox any reward he wanted, but Martin would take nothing for the help he had given Ian except his friendship. Then Ian Direach married the princess, and together they lived a long and happy life.

The King of the Crows

[FRANCE]

nce upon a time there lived a man who was as green as the grass, and who had only one eye, and that eye was in the middle of his forehead. The Green Man lived in an old house by the river in the forest of Ramier, and with him lived his three daughters. Each daughter was more beautiful than the other, and the youngest was the most beautiful of all.

One winter evening, just as night was falling, the Green Man sat by his window and watched the fog rise from the river. All of a sudden there came a beating of wings and a bird—big as a bull and black as night—came and perched on the window sill.

"Caw! Caw! Caw! I am the King of the Crows."

"What do you want from me?" asked the Green Man.

"Caw! Caw! Caw! Green Man, I wish to marry one of your three daughters."

"King Crow, wait here for me," said the Green Man, and he went to his daughters' room. "Listen, my daughters. The King of the Crows has come to demand one of you as his wife."

"Father," said the first daughter, "you know that I have been engaged for nearly a year to the King of Spain. Yesterday, my sweetheart sent me a message that he is coming soon to take me to his country. You see, Father, that I cannot marry the King of the Crows."

"Father," said the second daughter, "I have been engaged for nearly a year to the King of the Sea Islands. Yesterday my sweetheart sent me a message that he is coming soon to take me to his country. You see, Father, that I cannot marry the King of the Crows."

The Green Man looked at his third daughter. She was so young—not yet ten years old—that he took pity on her, and left the room without saying any more. He returned to his chamber where the King of the Crows awaited him. "King Crow," he said, "none of my daughters will accept you."

The King of the Crows flew into a terrible rage, and he pecked out the eye of the Green Man. Then he flew away into the fog.

The Green Man cried out in pain. His three daughters ran to him. "What has happened?" they cried. "Who has taken your eye?"

"It was the King of the Crows. He was angry because all three of you refused to marry him."

"Father," said the youngest, "I did not refuse to marry the King of the Crows."

"Very well," said their father. "Lead me to my

bed, and let no one enter my chamber unless I call."
The next evening, the Green Man summoned his
youngest daughter and said, "Take me to the room
where I sat last night when the King of the Crows
pecked out my eye. Open the window and leave
me there alone."

The girl did as her father asked. Night fell,
the fog rose up from the river, and the Green Man
sat by the window. There was a loud beating of
wings, and a bird—as big as a bull and as black as
pitch—flew down and perched on the window sill.

"Caw! Caw! Caw! I am King of the Crows."

"King Crow, what do you want from me?"
asked the Green Man.

"Caw! Caw! Caw! Green Man, I want to
marry one of your three daughters."

"King Crow, you may marry my youngest
daughter."

Then the King of the Crows restored the
Green Man's eye, and said, "Tell your daughter to
be ready tomorrow morning at dawn, with her
white dress and her wedding crown."

The next morning at sunrise, thousands of
crows darkened the sky. They alighted in front of
the house of the Green Man and set to work
preparing an altar for the wedding. At the foot of
the altar the King of the Crows lay covered by a
white sheet, like a shroud. When everything was
ready, and the candles had been lit, a priest
arrived—no one knew from where—to say the
mass. Then the priest disappeared as mysteriously
as he had come, and the King of the Crows
emerged from his shroud and said, "Take my bride

to her father, for she must prepare herself for the journey to my country."

At noon, the new queen stood in the doorway, ready to depart. "Goodbye, my father," she said. "Goodbye, sisters. I leave my house and land, and I shall never return."

Then the crows lifted her into the air and carried her to the land of cold and ice, the land where nothing green grows. By sundown, when they set the queen before the door of a great palace, they had flown three thousand miles.

"Thank you, crows," she said. "I will never forget your service. Go eat and sleep, for you have surely earned a rest."

The queen began to explore her new home. She found candles burning in every room and hallway, and fires glowing in all the fireplaces, but nowhere did she see a living soul. She came to a dining hall where she saw a table covered with food, but with only one place set. She sat down, yet she could not bring herself to eat, for she was thinking of her family and her home. So she went to the sleeping chamber, and lay down in a bed hung all around with curtains of gold and silver, and she left the candles burning.

On the first stroke of midnight, there was a beating of wings. The King of the Crows entered and stopped behind the chamber door, where she could not see him. "Put out the light!" he commanded. The queen put out the light, and the King of the Crows came into the room, and said to her, "Listen carefully to what I tell you. I was once a human king, but an evil magician enchanted me and all my court. It has been foretold that you have the power to rescue us. Every night I will come and sleep at your side. But you are young, and you will not be my wife for seven years. Until then, never try to see me, for if you do, great unhappiness will come to us."

"I will do as you say," the queen replied.

She heard the King of the Crows take off his feathered skin and lay down next to her. When she put out her hand toward him, she could feel the cold sharp blade of the sword that he had placed between them on the bed. The next morning, before dawn, the King of the Crows arose, took the sword, put on his feathered cloak, and flew away without saying a word.

From that day forward, it was the same every night and every morning, and the maiden found her life tedious and tiresome, for she never had anyone to talk to. Often she would leave the house early in the morning, carrying a basket of food, and walk across the ice and snow until dark. Never did she meet a living soul, until one morning when she was out walking and saw a high mountain that was clear of snow. She walked quickly toward the mountain, and she came at last to a tiny cabin by a stream. There an old washerwoman with skin like ancient leather knelt at the stream's edge, scrubbing cloth that was dirty as soot, and singing,

> *Fairy washerwoman,*
> *Your work shall be done,*
> *When the virgin queen has come.*

"Good day, washerwoman," said the queen. "I am going to help you with your work."

"Please do," said the old woman.

The queen had no sooner plunged the cloth into the water than it turned white as milk, and the washerwoman began to sing,

> *Fairy washerwoman,*
> *Your work is done,*
> *For the virgin queen has come.*

"I have been waiting for you for a long time," the old woman told the queen. "Now my work is done. But your suffering has not yet ended. Your husband gave you good advice, but advice is worth nothing when fate is involved. Come to me again on the day of your greatest need."

The queen returned to the castle and resumed her dreary life. Then, on the day before the seven years were to end, she said to herself, "My trials are nearly over. One day more, one day less, what does it matter? Tonight I will look at my husband as he sleeps."

Evening came. The queen lit a candle in the bedchamber, and she hid it so well that the room appeared totally dark. Then she lay down and waited. At the first stroke of midnight, there was a beating of wings. She heard the King of the Crows arrive and take off his feathered skin. Then he lay in bed, placed the sword between them, and went to sleep. The queen took the candle and held it up so that she could see her husband. There he lay, handsome as the day. She took a step toward the bed in order to see him better, but as she did so, she let a drop of hot wax fall upon his face.

"Oh, wife!" he cried. "You have caused a great evil for us all. Tomorrow, our trials would have been over, and I would have truly become your husband in my human shape. Now I must fall into the power of the evil magician. But what is done is done, and I forgive you for the harm you have caused. Leave this house, for you should not see the things that are about to happen here."

The queen left, sobbing. Then the magician came and wrapped the King of the Crows in a heavy chain and carried him to a high mountain on an island in the ocean. There the magician buried the end of the chain in a rock. He gave a whistle and two enormous wolves appeared, one white as snow, the other black as soot. The white wolf kept watch in the daytime and slept at night, while the black wolf kept watch at night and slept during the day. The magician departed, leaving the King of the Crows alone on the mountaintop.

Meanwhile the queen left the castle, and walked and walked, and cried until her eyes were dry, and after a long time she reached the place where she had met the old washerwoman.

"I see that you are unhappy," the woman said, "and I can guess why. Your husband is now a prisoner on an island in the sea. Here are some gifts that will help you to find him and free him." The old washerwoman gave the queen a pair of iron shoes to wear, and a flask in which she would always find something to drink, and a basket in which she would always find food. "Here is a golden knife," she said. "You must use it to cut the blue grass, the grass that sings night and day, the grass that breaks iron. And when at last your iron shoes are worn through, it will be time for you to free the King of the Crows."

The queen thanked the woman, and she set out upon her long journey. Three days later she came to the land where it is never night and the moon never shines, and she wandered there for a year. When she was hungry, she never failed to find food in the basket, and when she was thirsty, she never failed to find water in the flask. When she wanted to sleep, she lay down on the hard ground. And at the end of that year she found grass that was blue as the summer sky. She took her knife and began to cut.

"Do not cut me with your golden knife," said the grass. "Yes, I am blue, but I am not the grass that sings night and day, nor am I the grass that breaks iron."

The queen closed her knife and walked on. She came to the country where the sun is never seen but the moon always shines, and there she wandered for a year. When she was hungry, she found food in her basket, and whenever she was thirsty, she found water in her flask. When she became tired, she lay down on the hard ground and slept. And at the end of a year she found blue grass that was singing,

> *I am the blue grass,*
> *The grass that sings night and day.*

The queen took out her golden knife.

"Please, Queen! Do not cut me with your knife," cried the grass. "I am the blue grass, the grass that sings night and day. But I am not the grass that breaks iron."

The queen walked on, and she came to the country where neither the sun nor the moon shines, where it is always darkest night, and she wandered there for a year. When she was hungry or thirsty, food and drink were never lacking in her basket and her flask. When she was tired she lay down on the hard ground and slept. And at the end of a year she heard singing in the darkness,

> *I am the blue grass,*
> *The grass that sings night and day,*
> *The grass that breaks iron.*

She took out her golden knife and walked in the darkness toward the singing. Suddenly her iron shoes cracked, for she had stepped on the blue grass. The queen cut the grass, then she closed her knife and walked on, barefoot, through brambles and sharp pebbles. She walked long and far until at last the dark night ended and the sun rose. The queen found herself on the shore of the sea, and nearby she saw a small boat. She got into the boat and rowed out on the waves. For seven days and seven nights she saw nothing but sky and water.

On the morning of the eighth day, she came to the island where the King of the Crows was imprisoned. The white wolf rushed at her, and the queen waved the blue grass that sang,

I am the blue grass,
The grass that sings night and day,
The grass that breaks iron.

When he heard the singing, the white wolf lay down and fell asleep. The queen stabbed the white wolf with her golden knife, and likewise she stabbed the black wolf. She held out the blue grass and touched it to the chain that bound the King of the Crows, and the grass sang,

I am the blue grass,
The grass that sings night and day,
The grass that breaks iron.

The grass trembled and ceased singing, the chain broke, and the king arose in human form, strong and handsome.

Great flocks of crows arrived from the four corners of the sky, and as the crows touched ground, each took on human shape. And when they were all assembled, they looked out to sea. Thousands of boats were sailing from all directions to carry them back to their own country. The king and queen celebrated with great feasting, and they lived happily together to the end of their days.

The Enchanted Toad

[SWEDEN]

nce there lived a peasant who had three sons, and whose wife had died many years before. When the two elder lads were nearly grown, they went to their father and asked for his permission to go out into the world and find brides for themselves.

"It is not right that you look for brides before you have proven yourselves," said their father. "Go first and see which one of you can bring the finest cloth to spread on the table next Christmas."

The two brothers agreed at once to do this, and their father gave each of them five silver coins so that they could take care of themselves until they found work. On the evening before they were to leave home, the youngest son went to his father and begged him for permission to go and prove himself also. But his father wouldn't listen to him. "It is better that you stay at home and sit in the chimney corner," he said. "That is your place."

But the lad insisted, saying, "Father, let me go with them. Perhaps I shall succeed in the world even though I am smaller and younger than my brothers." The old man thought to himself that the boy would return home quickly enough, and so he let him follow his brothers, and gave him five silver coins to help him on his way.

The three sons set out, and toward evening they came to a tavern by the wayside. The two elder brothers went inside and ate and drank and gambled, while the youngest brother crept into a corner by himself and would not join in the merrymaking. After the two brothers had spent and gambled all their own money, they went to their younger brother, and demanded his five silver coins, and told him to go home. When the lad refused, his brothers beat him, and took his money, and chased him out of the tavern.

The youngest brother ran into the darkness, not knowing which way to go. He followed many rugged paths until he could go no further. Then he sat down on a small mound and wept bitterly until he fell asleep.

The next morning the lad awoke before the lark and continued his journey, walking over high mountains and through deep valleys, and at last he came to a green path that led to a house so large and beautiful, it seemed to him that it must be a royal palace. He entered the house and wandered through many rooms, each one more elegant than the last, but never did he see any living soul. He came at last to a room that was even more splendid than the others. There on a shining throne of gold and silver sat a toad so loathsome and so ugly that he could scarcely bear to look at it. The toad asked who he was and why he had come.

"I am a poor boy in search of honest work," he answered.

"I happen to be in need of a worker," said the toad. "Would you stay here and work for me?"

"Yes," the lad answered.

"Be welcome, then," said the toad, "and if you work faithfully, I will reward you with your heart's desire."

The lad followed her into the gardens that surrounded the house, and they came to a large bush of a kind he had never seen before.

"Your job will be to cut a branch of this bush every day while the sun is in the sky," said the toad. "Do this on Sunday as well as on Monday, on Christmas Day as well as on Midsummer Day. But you must never cut more than one branch a day."

The lad promised to do as she wished. Then the toad led him to the room where he would live, saying that on the table he would always find food and drink when he was hungry. He might do whatever he wished as long as he performed the task she had given him. The lad went into the garden and cut a branch from the bush, and the following morning, he did the same, and again on the third morning, and likewise for the rest of the year. And in his room he always found everything he wished for, but time passed slowly for him. Days came and days went, and he never saw or heard another human being.

When the year was at an end, and he had cut

the last branch of the bush, the toad came to him and thanked him for his faithful service. She asked what payment he would like. He said that he had done very little work, and would be satisfied with whatever she wished to give him.

"I know what you are seeking," said the toad. "Your brothers have gone in search of tablecloths to spread on your father's table this Yule Eve. But I will give you a cloth the like of which they will never find, even if they search through twelve kingdoms." And she gave him a cloth whiter than snow, and so finely woven it could pass through the eye of a needle. He thanked her and prepared to return to his father's house.

He traveled for several days, but not once did he see a house or a town, until one evening a light appeared in the distance. He walked toward it, hoping to find shelter for the night, and when he arrived he found himself at same tavern where he had left his brothers. There they sat, still eating, drinking and making merry. The lad was no longer angry at the way the two had treated him a year before, and so he greeted them warmly, and asked if they had found tablecloths to spread upon their father's Yule table.

Yes, the brothers answered, all had turned out very well for them. Then they showed him two tablecloths, and both were torn and dirty. "Wait until you see mine!" said their brother, and he spread his cloth out on the table. All the guests in the tavern gathered around to admire its color and texture, saying they had never seen anything like it. The two brothers could not bear to think that he should have found such a fine cloth, and so they took it for themselves, and made him take their old dirty tablecloths.

The three brothers returned home together, and when Yule Eve came the elder lads spread their youngest brother's cloth on the table. Wasn't the old man delighted! He could not praise his two sons enough, and they began to boast and to invent all sorts of fantastic things they had accomplished during the past year, and of course it was nothing but lies. The youngest brother said not a word. He knew his father would never believe him.

The two elder brothers went again to their father and begged for his permission to go and seek wives. But the old man answered that they should not be looking for brides before they had proven themselves a second time, and that they should bring back a drinking cup to set on the Yule table the following year. On their departure, the old man gave each one five silver coins as before.

When they had gone, the youngest lad went to his father and asked for permission to seek a drinking cup also. At first, his father refused, but later he gave in, thinking that the lad would surely give up and be back before spring. So the lad took his five silver coins and set out. He found his two brothers at the same tavern, eating, drinking and gambling, and of course they quickly robbed him of his money. Then he wandered off until he came at last to the palace of the toad, and she greeted him kindly.

"I have come to offer you my services again," he said, "if you are in need of a worker."

"It happens that I am just now in great need of a worker," the toad said, "and if you serve me well, your reward will be your heart's desire."

Then the toad took a bundle of short threads and gave them to the youth and said, "This will be your job. You will tie a thread around every branch of the bush you cut last year. You must tie a thread every day while the sun is in the sky, and you must do so on Sunday as well as on Monday, and on Christmas Day as well as on Midsummer Day. You must never tie many threads at once, but only one at a time."

When the year was at an end, and the youth had bound the last thread around the last branch, the toad came to him and asked what payment he wished for his service. He answered that he had done little to deserve a reward, and he would be happy with whatever she might give him.

"I know very well what reward you wish," said the toad. "Your brothers have set out to find a drinking cup to place on your father's table this Yule Eve. I will give you a cup the like of which is not to be found anywhere else in the world." And she gave him a silver drinking cup, gilded inside and out. Thirteen masters had set their marks upon it, and its equal would not have been found in a hundred kingdoms. The youth thanked her and prepared to return home.

After traveling several days, he came to the same tavern as before, and since there was no other shelter nearby, he stopped there for the night. He found his brothers sitting amid cups and jugs, just as they had been when he left them. Of course they once again robbed him of his treasure.

When the three brothers had been at home past Yule, the two elder ones went again to their father and asked his permission to set out in search of brides. The old man agreed to their request this time, thinking that his sons were now ready for marriage. "Return with a bride by next Yule Eve," he said, and he gave them their usual five coins.

The two brothers were about to leave, and the youngest son went to his father and begged to be allowed to go with them. "You poor bumbler," said the father. "Do you think there is any maiden in the world who would have you for a husband? Just sit at home by the fire and rake the ashes. That is the place for you."

The lad was not discouraged. "Father, let me go with them," he said. "No one can tell what may happen. Things may go well for me even though I am smaller and younger than my brothers." At last the old man thought he might as well say yes, for hunger would soon drive the boy home again.

The three brothers set out, and in the evening came to the tavern of which we have spoken more than once, where the usual scene was repeated. The elder brothers robbed the youngest and threw him out of doors. After long travels, the youth decided to try his luck again at the place where he had found such comfort and easy work before. He had scarcely thought this when he saw that he was walking once again on the green path that led to the toad's palace. He entered boldly into the throne room where the toad always sat, and she received him warmly and asked why he had come. He told her that he came to offer his services if she had need of them.

"You are welcome," said the toad, "for I am in great need of a worker. If you serve me well, your reward will be your heart's desire. This is what I ask of you. Gather up the branches you cut and tied, and lay them together in a heap in the courtyard. Take up one branch every day that the sun is in the sky, and do so on Wednesday as well as on Thursday, and on Christmas Day as well as on Midsummer Day, and you must not pick up many branches at one time, but a single one only. When the year is at an end, and you have gathered up the last branch, set fire to the heap. Then sweep around the pile so that every branch is burned completely. If you then see anything in the fire, take it out and keep it."

The youth promised to do as she asked. He went to the garden, took a branch that he had cut and tied before, and carried it to the courtyard. On the following morning he did the same, and again on the third morning, and so on through the year. In the palace he enjoyed every comfort as he grew to be a tall and handsome young man. But his hours were passed in solitude, for he did not see or hear another human being, and he often imagined that his brothers were living at home with their brides now, while he was all alone.

When the year had run its course, and the youth had gathered up the last branch and laid it with the others, he did as the toad had told him. He set fire to the heap, and swept around it until all the branches were burning. And behold! In the midst of the flames a beautiful maiden appeared. When the youth saw her, he rushed forward to pull her away from the fire. The maiden thanked him for saving her. She was a king's daughter, she told him, and long ago she had been enchanted by a troll and changed into a loathsome toad.

At that same moment there was a noise and a rustling as the palace courtyard was filled with dozens of servants and knights and damsels who had been disenchanted at that same moment.

The princess ordered that horses be harnessed to her chariot at once, and she had the peasant's son clothed in silk and scarlet, like a prince. "Now we shall travel to see your father, so that he may know what kind of bride you have earned for yourself," she said.

Soon the royal chariot arrived at the peasant's cottage, and the young man and his bride asked the old man for shelter for the night, without revealing their true identities. He told them that he did not have any rooms suitable for royal persons such as themselves. But the princess insisted, and at last he agreed. She ordered her servants to prepare a sumptuous Yule feast, and sent messengers to invite everyone who lived nearby to come and share it with them.

Later that evening, the two brothers arrived with their brides, and the old man was not at all pleased with his new daughters-in-law, who were women of the worst sort. After all the guests had arrived for the feast, the princess admired the beautiful tablecloth and magnificent drinking cup, and she asked the man where they had come from.

He answered that he had gotten them from his two elder sons.

"Not true," said the princess, "for neither one of those two has earned such treasures, but my husband has."

Then the youth revealed who he was, and told how his brothers had robbed and cheated him. The brothers turned pale and were shamed in front of everyone, and when the Yule feast was over, they ran away and were never heard of again. The princess and the peasant's son returned to her kingdom, taking his father with them. The youth became king over the whole realm and lived long with his queen in love and harmony.

Oh,
the Tsar of the Forest

[UKRAINE]

ong long ago, before our great-grandparents or their parents had been born into the world, there lived a poor man and his wife, and they had one son who did not behave as an only son should. He would do nothing. He would not even fetch water from the well, but merely lay on the stove all day long and rolled among the warm cinders. He was twenty years old, yet he just sat on the stove without any trousers on. If his parents gave him something to eat, he ate it, and if they gave him nothing to eat, he didn't complain. His father and mother said, "What are we to do with you, son? You are good for nothing. Other people's children comfort and help their parents, but you are a fool. You eat our bread and do nothing in return." But their complaints were of no use at all. The lad would do nothing but sit on the stove and play with the cinders.

At last his mother said to his father, "What is to be done with our son? He has grown up and yet he is of no use to us. If we can hire him out, let us hire him out. Perhaps someone else will be able to do more with him than we have." So his father and mother sent him to a tailor's to learn tailoring. There he remained three days before he ran home again, climbed on the stove, and began playing in the ashes. His father gave him a sound drubbing and then sent him to a cobbler's to learn cobbling, but again the son ran home. His father gave him another drubbing and sent him to a blacksmith to learn smith's work. But he did not remain there long before he ran home again. What was that poor father to do?

"I'll tell you what I'll do with you, you lazy lout," said he. "I'll take you to another kingdom where perhaps someone will be able to teach you better than we can here—and it will be so far away that you won't be able to run home."

So they set out, and they walked until at last they entered a forest so dark that they could see neither earth nor sky. They grew weary, and when they came to a clearing full of large tree stumps, the father said, "I am so tired out that I will rest here a little," and with that he sat down on a tree stump. "Oh!" he said. "How tired I am!"

No sooner had he spoken these words than out of the stump sprang a little old man, all wrinkled and puckered. His beard was quite green, and it reached right down to his knees.

"Well, since you have called me, what do you want of me?" asked the strange man.

The lad's father was astonished and replied, "I certainly did *not* call you. Be gone!"

"How can you deny that you called me?" shrieked the little old man. "I am Oh, the Tsar of the Forest. Why did you call me?"

"Away with you! I did not call you," said the lad's father.

"What? Are you saying that you were not calling me when you said 'Oh'?"

"I was tired, and that is why I said 'Oh'," answered the man.

"And what business brings you here?"

The man sighed. "I am taking this scurvy blockhead of mine to hire him out to somebody or other, in hopes that someone may be able to knock more sense into him than we can at home. No matter where we send him, he always comes running home again."

"Hire him out to me. I promise I'll teach him a thing or two," said Oh. "Yet I'll only take him on one condition. You must come back for him at the end of a year, and if you recognize him again, I will return him to you. But if you do not recognize him, he shall serve another year with me."

"Good!" cried the man.

So they shook hands, and the man went back to his own home. Oh took the son away with him, and they passed into the other world beneath the earth. Soon they came to a hut woven of rushes. In this hut everything was green. The walls were green, and the benches were green, and Oh's wife and children were green. And Oh had water nixies for serving maids that were all as green as rue.

"Sit down," said Oh. "Have a bite of something to eat." The nixies brought him food that was also green, and he ate it. "And now," Oh told the nixies, "take this lad into the courtyard so that he may chop wood and draw water from the well."

The nixies took the lad into the courtyard, but instead of chopping wood, he simply lay down and went to sleep. Oh came out to check on him, and there he lay snoring. Oh seized him by the ear, and told the nixies to bring wood, and tie the boy to it, and set the wood on fire until the lad was burnt to ashes, and they did. Then Oh took the ashes and scattered them to the four winds. As he did so, a single piece of burnt coal fell from among the ashes. Oh sprinkled this coal with water from the well, and there stood the lad alive and well, somewhat handsomer and a bit stronger than before.

Again Oh told him to chop wood, but again the lad went to sleep. Then Oh tied him to the wood, and burned him, and scattered the ashes to the four winds, and sprinkled the one remaining coal with living water. And instead of the former lazy lout, there stood before him such a handsome and stalwart hero as can only be imagined or described in fairy tales.

The lad remained there for a year, and at the end of the year his father came for him. The man found that same clearing in the forest, and sat down, and said "Oh!"

The Tsar of the Forest immediately came out of the tree stump and asked, "What do you want?"

"I have come for my son."

"Follow me, then," said Oh, "and if you can

recognize him, you shall take him home. But if you cannot recognize him, he will remain with me for another year."

So the man followed Oh to his hut, and Oh took handfuls of millet seed and scattered it on the ground. Dozens of roosters came running to eat it. "Well, do you recognize your son?" asked Oh. The man stared and stared. To him, one rooster looked just like another. He could not recognize his son. "Well," said Oh, "since you do not recognize him, go home, for your son must remain in my service another year."

The second year passed, and the father came again to the clearing in the forest, sat on a stump and said, "Oh!"

Oh popped out of the tree stump saying, "Come and see if you recognize him now." Then he took the father to a sheep pen where there were rows upon rows of rams, one just like another. The man tried, but he could not decide which one was his son. "You may as well go home then," said Oh. "Your son must stay with me one more year." So the man went away, and he was very sad at heart, for he had begun to wonder if he would ever see his son again.

A third year passed, and the father set out once more to find Oh. On his way, he met an old man dressed in glistening white clothing. The man greeted him and asked where he was going. "I am trying to free my son from Oh, the Tsar of the Forest," said the father, and he told the man how he had placed his son in Oh's service, and how he had been unable to release him.

"Yes, yes," said the man, "Oh will lead you around by the nose for a long time."

And since the man seemed to know something about the matter, the lad's father asked, "Can you tell me how I may recover my son? For though he has not been much good to me, he is still my own flesh and blood."

"Pay attention," said the old man. "When you find Oh, he will set loose a flock of doves before you, but your son will not be among them. He will be the dove that does not come out, but remains sitting beneath the pear tree preening its feathers. That will be your son."

The father thanked the man in white and went on. He came to the clearing in the forest and said, "Oh!" Oh appeared and led him to his forest kingdom. He scattered wheat upon the ground and called to his doves, and so many birds appeared that there was no counting them, and each dove looked just like the others.

"Do you recognize your son?" asked Oh. "If you do, he is yours again. If you do not, he is mine forever."

Now, all the doves there were pecking at the wheat except one that sat alone beneath a pear tree preening its feathers. The man pointed to it. "That is my son," he said.

"You have found him, so take him!" shouted Oh angrily.

Then the father reached out to the dove, and immediately it changed into a handsome young man. His father embraced and kissed him. "Let us go home, my son," said he. And as they traveled along the road together, they fell to talking. The father asked his son how he had gotten along in Oh's kingdom, and the son told him. Then the father said, "What shall we do now, my son? I am poor and you are poor. Have you worked these three years and earned nothing?"

"Don't worry, dear father," said the son. "I have earned little but learned much. Do you see those three young noblemen hunting a fox? I will turn myself into a greyhound and catch the fox, so that they will want to buy me. You must sell me to them for three hundred rubles—only be sure to sell me without a chain. Then we shall have lots of money and live happily together."

The son changed himself into a greyhound and quickly ran down the fox. The noblemen came galloping out of the forest to where the man stood.

"Is that your greyhound?" they demanded.

"It is."

"What a fine dog. What will you take for it?"

"Three hundred rubles without the chain."

"We don't need your chain. We will give him a chain of gold," they all laughed. "Here is your money. Now give us the dog."

They sent the dog after another fox and quick as a flash he chased the beast into the forest. Then he turned into a youth again and rejoined his father. As they walked along, the father said, "This money is barely enough to begin to repair our hut."

"Don't worry, Father. I see three nobles hunting quail with falcons. I will change into a falcon, and you will sell me to them for three hundred rubles—but be sure to sell me without the hood."

They watched the young noblemen cast their falcon at a quail. The falcon pursued, but always fell short of the quail, and the quail always escaped from the falcon. Then the son became a falcon and immediately struck down the prey.

The young noblemen were amazed. "Is that your falcon?" they asked the father.

"It is."

"Sell it to us, then. What do you want for it?"

"If you pay three hundred rubles, you may have it, but it must be bought without the hood."

"As if we wanted your hood! We'll give it a hood worthy of a tsar," said the noblemen. They gave him three hundred rubles, and then they sent the falcon after another quail, and it flew and flew until it disappeared into the trees. Then he became a youth again and rejoined his father.

"We still have very little money," lamented the father.

"Wait a bit and we shall have more," said the son, "for I see a fair up ahead. When we get there I will change myself into a horse so that you can sell me. Someone will give you a thousand rubles for me, only be sure to sell me without a halter."

When they got to the fair, the son changed himself into a horse, a horse as supple as a serpent, and so fiery that it was dangerous to approach him. The father led the horse along by the halter, and it pranced and struck sparks from the ground with its hooves. Then the horse dealers came together and began to bargain for it.

"A thousand rubles buys the horse," said the father, "but without the halter."

"What do we want with your halter? We will make it a halter of silver and gold. Come, we will give five hundred rubles."

"No," said the father.

Then along came a strange old man who was blind in one eye. "How much do you want for this horse?" he asked.

"A thousand rubles without the halter."

"Nay, but that is too much. Will you take five hundred with the halter?"

"No!"

"Take six hundred, then." The old man began higgling and haggling, but still the father would not give way.

"Come, sell it to me with the halter," the old man pleaded.

"No, I have a liking for that halter."

"But, my good man, when did you ever see a horse sold without a halter? How can a person lead him off then?"

"The halter must remain mine," insisted the father.

"Look now, this is my last offer. I will give you a thousand rubles, and five rubles more, and I must have the halter."

The father fell to thinking that the halter was worth almost nothing, yet the old man offered him five rubles for it, so he sold the horse to the old man with the halter. They clinched the bargain with a good drink. The father went home with the money, and the old man walked off with the horse. But it was not really an old man at all. It was Oh, the Tsar of the Forest.

Oh rode off on the horse, and the horse rose into the air and carried him higher than the tree-tops. At last they sank down among the woods and came to Oh's forest dwelling. Oh went into his hut and tied the horse outside.

"This son of a dog shall not escape from my hands so quickly a second time," said Oh. And at dawn Oh took the horse by the bridle and led it to the river to drink. But no sooner did the horse get to the river and bend down its head to drink than it turned into a perch and began swimming away. Instantly Oh turned himself into a pike and swam after the perch.

But just as the pike had almost caught up with it, the perch gave a sudden twist and stuck out its spiky fins and turned its tail towards the pike, so that the pike could not lay hold of it. So when the pike came up to it, it said, "Perch! Perch! Turn your head towards me. I want to have a chat with you."

"I can hear you very well from here, dear cousin, if you want to chat," answered the perch.

So off they swam, and the pike overtook the perch. "Perch, perch, turn your head toward me. I want to have a chat with you."

Then the perch stuck out its bristly fins again and said, "If you wish to have a chat, dear cousin, I can hear you just as well as I am."

So the pike kept on pursuing the perch, but it was of no use. At last the perch swam ashore, and there sat a tsarina whittling an ash twig. The perch changed itself into a gold ring set with garnets, and the tsarina saw it and fished up the ring out of the water. Full of joy, she took it home. "Look, papa, what a beautiful ring I have found!" she said as she tried to decide which of her fingers it would look best on.

About the same time, a merchant came to the tsar and said, "I was sailing on the sea, and I had in my possession a precious garnet ring that was to be a gift for the tsar of my own land, but I dropped the ring into the water. Has any of your servants perchance found it?"

"No, but my daughter has," said the tsar. So they called the tsarina, and the merchant begged her to give it back, saying that his life would be in danger if he did not take it to his tsar. But it was no use. She refused to give it up.

Then her father pleaded with her, "Give it up, for it will be an evil thing if misfortune comes to this man because of us."

"Ask whatever you wish of me," the merchant said, "only give me back the ring."

"Nay then!" said the tsarina, "it shall neither be yours nor mine." And with that she threw the ring to the ground where it turned into a heap of millet seed and scattered all over the floor. Then the merchant (who, as you have probably guessed, was Oh, the Tsar of the Forest, in disguise) became a rooster and pecked up all of the millet. But one single grain of millet rolled right beneath the foot of the tsarina, and he did not see that one. The rooster jumped up onto the window sill, opened his wings, and flew away.

Then the one remaining grain of millet turned into a young man so radiantly handsome that the tsarina fell in love with him on the spot, and begged the tsar and tsaritsa to let her marry him.

"I shall never be happy with any other man," said she. "My happiness is with him alone!" For a long time, her parents refused, but at last they gave them their blessing. The two young people were crowned with bridal wreaths and everyone in the tsardom was invited to the wedding feast.

The Firebird
and the Horse of Power

[RUSSIA]

nce upon a time, a powerful tsar ruled in a country far away. And among his servants was a young archer. This archer had a horse—a horse of power—such a horse as belonged to the wonderful men of long ago—a great horse with a broad chest, eyes like fire, and hooves of iron. One day, in the spring of the year, this young archer rode alone through the forest on his horse of power. All the trees were green, and squirrels ran among the branches, and hares leapt through the undergrowth, but, strangely, no birds sang. The young archer rode along the forest path and listened for the singing of the birds, but there was no singing. The only noises in the forest were the scratchings of four-footed beasts, the dropping of fir cones upon the ground, and the heavy stamping of the horse of power on the soft path. "What could have happened to the birds?" the young archer wondered.

He had scarcely said this when he saw a large curved feather lying on the path before him. The feather was bigger than a swan's, bigger than an eagle's. It lay on the path, glittering like a flame, for the sun was shining on it, and the feather was of pure gold. Then the archer knew why there was no singing in the forest, for the feather was that of the firebird.

The horse of power spoke and said, "Leave that golden feather where it lies, for if you take it, you will be sorry, and you will understand the meaning of fear."

The brave young archer sat on the horse of power and looked at the golden feather, and wondered whether to take it or not. He had no wish to learn what it was to be afraid, but he thought, "If I take it and bring it to the tsar, he will be pleased, and will not send me away empty-handed, for no tsar in the world has a feather from the burning breast of the firebird." And the more he thought about it, the more he wanted to take the feather to the tsar. So in the end he did not listen to the words of the horse of power. He leapt from the saddle, picked up the golden feather, mounted his horse again, and galloped back through the green forest until he came to the palace.

He went into the palace, and bowed low and said, "O Tsar, I have brought you a feather of the firebird."

The tsar looked gladly at the feather, and then at the young archer. "Thank you," said the tsar, "but if you have brought me a feather of the firebird, surely you will be able to bring me the bird itself. I should like to see it. A mere feather is not a fitting gift to bring to the tsar. Bring the bird itself or, I swear by my sword, your head shall no longer sit between your shoulders."

The young archer bowed his head and went out. Bitterly he wept, for he had begun to know what it was to be afraid. He went out into the courtyard, where the horse of power was waiting for him, tossing its head and stamping the ground.

"Master," said the horse of power, "why do you weep?"

"The tsar has told me to bring him the firebird, and no one on earth can do that," said the archer, and he hung his head.

"I told you," said the horse of power, "that if you took the feather you would learn the meaning of fear. Well, do not be frightened—yet—and do not weep. The trouble is not now. The trouble lies before you. Go to the tsar and ask him to have a hundred sacks of grain scattered over the open field, and let this be done at midnight."

The young archer went back into the palace and begged the tsar to do this, and the tsar ordered that at midnight a hundred sacks of grain should be scattered in the open field.

Next morning, the young archer rode out on the horse of power, and came to the open field. The ground was scattered all over with grain. In the middle of the field stood a great oak. The young archer leapt to the ground, took off the saddle, and let the horse of power loose to wander as he pleased about the field. Then he climbed up into the oak and hid himself among the green boughs.

The sky grew red and gold, and the sun rose. Suddenly there was a noise in the forest around the field. The trees shook and swayed, and almost fell. There was a mighty wind. The sea piled itself into waves with crests of foam, and the firebird came flying from the other side of the world. Huge and golden and flaming in the sun, it flew, dropped down with open wings into the field, and began to eat the grain.

The horse of power wandered in the field. This way he went, and that, but always he came a little nearer to the firebird. Nearer and nearer came the horse. He came close up to the firebird, and then suddenly stepped on one of its spreading fiery wings and pressed it heavily to the ground. The bird struggled, flapping mightily with its fiery wings, but it could not get away. The young archer slipped down from the tree, bound the firebird with three strong ropes, swung it on his back, saddled the horse, and rode to the palace of the tsar.

The young archer stood before the tsar, and his back was bent under the great weight of the firebird, and the broad wings of the bird hung on either side of him like fiery shields, and there was a trail of golden feathers on the floor. The young archer swung the magic bird to the foot of the throne before the tsar, and the tsar was glad, because since the beginning of the world no tsar had seen the firebird flung before him like a wild duck caught in a snare.

The tsar looked at the firebird and laughed with pride. Then he lifted his eyes and looked at the young archer, and said, "Since you were able to capture the firebird, you will surely know how to bring me my bride. In the land of Never, on the very edge of the world, where the red sun rises in flame from the sea, lives Princess Vasilisa. Bring her to me, and I will reward you with silver and gold. But if you do not bring her, then your head will no longer sit between your shoulders!"

The young archer wept bitter tears, and went out into the courtyard where the horse of power was stamping the ground with its hooves of iron and tossing its thick mane.

"Master, why do you weep?" asked the horse of power.

"The tsar has ordered me to go to the land of Never, and bring back the Princess Vasilisa," the archer replied.

"Do not weep and do not grieve. The trouble is not yet. The trouble is to come. Go to the tsar and ask him for a silver tent with a golden roof, and for all kinds of food and drink to take with us on the journey."

The young archer went in and asked the tsar for this, and the tsar gave him a silver tent with a gold-embroidered roof, and every kind of rich wine, and the tastiest of foods.

Then the young archer mounted the horse of power and rode off to the land of Never. On and on he rode, many days and nights, and came at last to the edge of the world, where the red sun rises in flame from behind the deep blue sea.

On the shore of the sea the young archer reined in the horse of power, and the heavy hooves of the horse sank in the sand. He shaded his eyes and looked out over the blue water, and there was the Princess Vasilisa in a little silver boat, rowing with golden oars.

The young archer rode back a little way to where the sand ended and the green world began. There he set the horse loose to wander wherever he pleased, and to feed on the green grass. Then on the edge of the shore, where the green grass ended and grew thin and the sand began, he set up the shining tent. In the tent he set out the tasty dishes and the rich flagons of wine which the tsar had given him, and he sat himself down in the tent and began to regale himself while he waited for the Princess Vasilisa.

The Princess Vasilisa dipped her golden oars in the blue water, and the little silver boat moved lightly through the dancing waves. She sat in the little boat and looked over the blue sea to the edge of the world, and there, between the golden sand and the green earth, she saw the tent shining silver and gold in the sun. She dipped her oars and came nearer in order to see it better. The nearer she came, the more beautiful the tent seemed, and at last she rowed to shore and landed her little boat on the sand, and walked up to the tent. She was a little frightened, and now and again she stopped and looked back to where the silver boat lay on the sand with the blue sea beyond it. The young archer said not a word, but feasted upon the pleasant dishes he had set out there in the tent. At last the Princess Vasilisa came up to the tent and looked in.

The young archer rose and bowed to her and said, "Good day to you, Princess. Be so kind as to come in and take bread and salt with me, and taste my foreign wines."

And the Princess Vasilisa came into the tent and sat down with the young archer, and ate sweetmeats with him, and drank his health in a golden goblet of the wine the tsar had given him. Now this wine was heavy, and the last drop from the goblet had no sooner trickled down her slender throat than her eyes closed against her will once, twice, and again.

"Ah me!" said the Princess. "I feel as if night itself had perched on my eyelids, and yet it is barely noon."

The golden goblet dropped to the ground from her fingers, and she leaned back on a cushion and fell asleep. Quickly the young archer called to the horse of power. Lightly he lifted the princess in his strong arms. Swiftly he leapt with her into the saddle. Like a feather she lay in the hollow of his left arm, and slept while the iron hooves of the great horse thundered over the ground.

They came to the tsar's palace, and the young archer leapt from the horse of power and carried the princess inside. Great was the joy of the tsar, but it did not last for long.

"Go, sound the trumpets for our wedding," he said to his servants. "Let all the bells be rung."

The bells rang out and the trumpets sounded, and at the noise of the horns and the ringing of the bells the Princess Vasilisa woke up and looked about her.

"What is this ringing of bells," said she, "and this noise of trumpets? And where is the blue sea, and my little silver boat with its golden oars?"

"The blue sea is far away," said the tsar, "and in exchange for your little silver boat I give you a golden throne. The trumpets sound for our wedding, and the bells are ringing for our joy."

But the Princess turned her face away from the tsar, and there was no wonder in that, for he was old, and his eyes were not kind. And she looked with love at the young archer, and there was no wonder in that either, for he was a young man fit to ride the horse of power.

The tsar was angry. "Why, Princess," said he, "will you not marry me, and forget your blue sea and your silver boat?"

"In the middle of the deep blue sea lies a great stone," said the princess, "and under that stone is hidden my wedding dress. If I cannot wear that dress, I will marry nobody at all."

The tsar turned to the young archer, who was waiting before the throne. "Return to the land of Never," said he, "and find the great stone that lies in the middle of the sea, and bring me Princess Vasilisa's wedding dress. If you do not, your head shall no longer sit between your shoulders."

The young archer wept bitter tears, and went out into the courtyard, where the horse of power was waiting for him, champing its golden bit.

"Master, why do you weep?" asked the horse of power.

"The tsar has ordered me to fetch Princess Vasilisa's wedding dress from the bottom of the sea. I weep also because the dress is for the tsar's wedding, yet I love the Princess Vasilisa myself."

"What did I tell you?" said the horse of power. "I told you that there would be trouble if you picked up the golden feather of the firebird. Well, do not be afraid. The trouble is not yet. The trouble is to come. Up into the saddle with you, and away for the wedding dress of the Princess Vasilisa!"

The young archer looked sadly over the wide waters, but the horse of power tossed its mane and did not look at the sea, but at the shore. This way and that it looked, and saw at last a huge lobster moving slowly along the sand. Nearer and nearer came the lobster—it was the tsar of all the lobsters—and it moved slowly along the shore, while the horse of power moved carefully until it stood between the lobster and the sea. Then the horse of power lifted an iron hoof and set it firmly on the lobster's tail.

"Let me live!" screamed the lobster. "I will do whatever you ask of me!"

"Very well," said the horse of power. "We will let you live." Slowly he lifted his hoof. "But this is what you shall do for us. In the middle of the sea is a great stone, and under that stone lies the wedding dress of the Princess Vasilisa. Bring it here."

The lobster cried out in a voice that could be heard all over the deep blue sea, and the sea bubbled and churned, and from all sides lobsters by the thousands made their way toward the bank. The tsar of the lobsters ordered them to find the wedding dress of the Princess Vasilisa, and after a little time the sea bubbled and churned, and lobsters by the thousands came to the shore, and with them they brought a golden casket, and in it lay the wedding dress of the Princess Vasilisa.

The young archer took the golden casket, and the horse of power turned about and galloped back to the tsar's palace. The archer gave the casket into the hands of the princess, and looked at her with great sadness. Then the princess clothed herself in the dress, and she was fairer than the springtime, and the joy of the tsar was great. The wedding feast was made ready. Bells rang, and flags waved above the palace.

But the Princess Vasilisa refused to take the hand of the tsar. "I will marry nobody," she said, "until the man who brought me here has done penance in boiling water."

The tsar turned at once to his servants and ordered them to make a fire and to fill a cauldron with water and set it on the fire, and when the water was hot, to take the young archer and throw him into it.

"Oh misery!" cried the archer. "Why did I ever take the golden feather that had fallen from the firebird's burning breast? Why did I not listen to the wise words of the horse of power?" And, remembering his wise horse, the archer begged the tsar to let him see his horse one more time.

"Very well," said the tsar. "Say goodbye to your horse, for you will not ride him again. But let your farewell be short, for we are waiting."

The young archer crossed the courtyard and came to the horse of power, who was scraping the ground with his iron hooves. "Farewell, my horse of power," said the young archer. "I should have listened to your words, for now the end is come. The tsar has ordered that I am to be thrown into that cauldron that is seething on the great fire."

"Fear not," said the horse of power, "for the Princess Vasilisa has made him do this, and the end of these things is better than I thought. Go back, and when they are ready to throw you in the cauldron, run boldly and leap into the water."

The young archer went back across the courtyard, and the servants made ready to throw him into the cauldron.

"Is the water boiling yet?" asked the Princess Vasilisa.

"It bubbles and seethes," said the servants.

"Let me see for myself," said the princess, and she went to the fire and waved her hand above the cauldron. And some say there was something in her hand, and some say there was not.

"It is boiling," said she, and the servants laid hands on the young archer. But he struggled free of them, and he leapt into the very middle of the cauldron. Twice he sank below the surface, borne round with the bubbles and foam of the boiling water. Then he jumped from the cauldron and stood before the tsar and the princess, and he had become so beautiful a youth that all who saw him cried aloud in wonder.

"This is a miracle," cried the tsar. He looked at the handsome young archer and thought of his own bent back, and his gray beard, and his toothless gums. "I too will become beautiful," said he. He rose from his throne and climbed into the cauldron, where he was boiled to death in a moment.

And the end of the story? They buried the tsar, and made the young archer tsar in his place. He married the Princess Vasilisa, and lived many years with her in love and good fellowship. And he built a golden stable for the horse of power, and never forgot what he owed to him.

Prince Unexpected

[POLAND]

 king and queen had been married for three years, but they had no children. One day, the king set out on a tour of his dominions, and stayed away for many months. As he was riding across a great deserted plain in the heat of summer, the king was overcome by thirst. He sent his servants to look for water, and though they searched for hours, they could find none. Tormented by thirst, the king himself began to look. He rode on until he came to a well that was full to the brim with water, and on the water floated a silver cup with a golden handle. The king sprang down from his horse and reached out for the cup. But the cup, just as if it were alive, darted away. "I can drink just as well without the cup," the king said, and he knelt down and began to sip water from his hands. As he did so, his long beard dipped into the water, and when he tried to stand up, something had hold of his beard and wouldn't let it go. He pulled again and again, but it was no use.

"Let go, whoever you are!" the king shouted.

"I, Bony, king of the Underworld, have got your beard, and I won't let go until you promise to give me that thing which you left unknowingly at home, and which you do not expect to find on your return."

The king looked into the well, and there he saw a horrid head with green eyes and a grin that stretched from ear to ear. Hands with claws like a crab were holding his beard. The king quickly decided that a thing he had left at home and did not expect to find on his return could not be very valuable and so he said, "You shall have it."

The face in the water burst into laughter and vanished, and at the same time the well, the water, and the cup disappeared, and the king was left kneeling on dry sand. He got up, crossed himself, sprang onto his horse, hastened to his join his servants, and rode on.

In a month or so the king returned to the palace. There stood the queen holding a cushion, and on the cushion lay a child as beautiful as the moon. The king sighed painfully and thought, "So this is what I left without knowing and found without expecting," and he wept, but no one dared ask why. People noticed that the king was not as cheerful as before, but they did not know the cause.

Weeks, months, and years passed. The child, who was named Prince Unexpected, grew into a handsome youth. The king slowly regained his former cheerfulness, and forgot what had taken place that day by the well. But someone else had not forgotten. One day, when Prince Unexpected was hunting in the forest, he became separated from his companions and lost his way. All of a sudden, a monstrous old man with green eyes appeared in front of him.

"How do you do, Prince Unexpected. You have made me wait a long time for you."

"Who are you?" asked the prince.

"You will find that out soon enough," said the old man. "Please tell your father I send him my respects, and tell him that if he does not keep his promise to me, he will be sorry."

Then the hideous old man disappeared. Prince Unexpected rode home and told the king what had happened. The king turned pale as death. Then he revealed the horrible secret to his son.

"Don't worry, Father," said the prince. "It isn't such a great misfortune. I will force Bony to give up his rights to me because he tricked you in such a dishonest way. But if I do not return to you within a year, it will be a sign that we shall see one another no more."

The king gave his son a suit of steel armor, a sword, and a horse, and the queen hung a cross of pure gold around his neck. They hugged one another and wept, and then the prince rode off.

He rode one day, two days, three days, and at sunset on the fourth day he came to the ocean. There he saw twelve snow-white dresses on the beach, though not a living soul was in sight, only twelve white geese swimming far from shore.

Prince Unexpected wanted to know where the owners of the dresses were, so he took one of them, let his horse loose in a meadow, hid himself behind a tree, and waited to see what would happen. After splashing in the water, the geese swam to shore. Eleven of them went to the dresses. Each threw herself on the ground and became a beautiful maiden and ran away. The twelfth and last did not dare come up on the shore, but only stretched her neck out sadly, looking all around. Then she saw the prince and called out, "Give me my dress, Prince Unexpected, and I will be grateful to you." The prince placed her dress gently on the grass and turned his eyes away as she dressed herself and changed into a maiden, younger and more beautiful than the others.

"I am the youngest daughter of immortal King Bony," she told the prince. "My father has been expecting you for a long time, and he is very angry. Do not be frightened, but do as I tell you. As soon as you see King Bony, fall at once to your knees, and pay no attention to his shouts and threats. Approach him boldly. What will happen then, you will soon learn. Now we must part."

Then the princess stamped her foot on the ground. The ground sprang open, and the two of them descended into the underground, and Prince Unexpected found himself standing in front of a palace that shone brighter than our sun. He advanced boldly into the main hall. There sat Bony on a golden throne with a glittering crown on his head. His eyes gleamed like two saucers of green glass, and his fingers snapped like the nippers of a crab. As soon as he saw Bony, the prince fell to his knees. Bony gave a terrifying shout, but Prince Unexpected moved steadily forward on his knees, and when he was only a few steps from Bony's throne, the king smiled.

"You have amused me, and that is your good fortune," said the king. "I will allow you to remain in my kingdom if you perform three tasks I give you. But it is late, and we will begin tomorrow. Go to your room."

Prince Unexpected was led to a room, and the next morning King Bony summoned him and said, "Let us see what skills you possess. Build me a palace of pure marble, with windows of crystal, and a roof of gold, surrounded by a garden and fountains, and do so by tomorrow morning. If you succeed, you will gain my respect. If not, I will order that your head be cut off."

The prince returned to his room where he sat mournfully thinking of the death that awaited him. Then he heard a bee buzzing outside the window. "Let me in," said a small voice. He opened the lattice, the bee flew in, and Bony's youngest daughter appeared before him. "What is on your mind, Prince Unexpected?" she asked.

"Your father wishes my death," the prince said, and he told her of Bony's command.

"Don't be afraid," said the princess. "Lie down and sleep, and when you get up tomorrow morning, the palace will be built." And so it came to pass. At dawn the next morning, when the prince looked out his window, there stood the most beautiful palace he had ever seen.

"Well," said King Bony when he saw the palace, "you have succeeded this time. This will be your second task. Tomorrow I will call my twelve daughters before you. Unless you can guess which one is the youngest, your head will roll beneath the executioner's axe."

Later, the prince sat in his room, quite happy and contented, saying to himself, "Of course I will recognize the youngest princess!"

"Perhaps you won't," said the princess, flying into the room in the shape of a bee. "If I don't help you, you will never recognize me, for my sisters and I are so alike that even our father can only tell us apart by our clothing. But you will know me by the tiny ladybug that sits over my eyebrow. Look closely! Farewell."

Early the next morning, King Bony summoned Prince Unexpected to the throne room, and there stood twelve princesses, all dressed alike, their eyes cast down. The prince walked past them once, twice, then a third time, and only then did he see a ladybug perched above the eyebrow of one of the princesses. "This one is the youngest," said Prince Unexpected.

"How have you guessed?" cried King Bony angrily. "There must be some trickery going on here. I see that I will need to treat you differently than other princes who have come here. Return in three hours and prove your powers to me while I watch. I will light a straw, and you must cut and stitch a pair of boots before it goes out. If you fail, you will perish."

The prince returned sadly to his room, and found that the princess awaited him. "What am I to do?" he asked. "I am not a cobbler. Even if I were, I could never stitch a pair of boots that fast."

"No," the princess agreed, "the only thing we can do now is to escape together."

She spat on the window, and the spittle froze solid. Then she left the room with the prince, locked the door after them, and threw the key far away. They held hands and rose up into the air, and in an instant they found themselves at the very spot where they had entered the underground kingdom, and the prince's well-fed horse awaited them. The prince mounted his horse, the princess seated herself behind him, and off they rode as swiftly as an arrow.

At the appointed time, King Bony's servants went to fetch the prince in his chamber. "I'll come soon," said a voice from his room. The servants carried this answer to the king, who waited and waited, but the prince did not come. Bony sent his servants again, and again the voice told them, "I'll come soon." They carried this message to the king.

"What?" roared King Bony. "Does he mean to make fun of me? Go at once, break down the door, and bring him to me."

The servants hurried and broke down the door, and to their surprise, they found the room empty. Bony nearly burst with rage when they told him. He ordered his army to ride after his daughter and Prince Unexpected, and he threatened them with death if they returned empty-handed.

The prince and the princess were riding swiftly when they heard a noise behind them. "Someone is coming after us!" the prince cried. Instantly the princess changed herself into a river, and the prince into a bridge, and the horse into a raven. And she made the road beyond the bridge split into three roads. After the riders crossed the bridge, they did not know which way to go, and in their confusion they returned to Bony's palace.

"A bridge and a river?" shouted Bony. "That was Prince Unexpected and my daughter! Go back, and this time do not return without them."

Again, the prince and princess heard the sound of riders pursuing them, and this time the princess turned herself and the prince and the horse into a dark and gloomy forest full of roads and footpaths without number, and made it seem as if two riders were riding through it. On and on the riders chased this illusion, only to find themselves right where they had started. So they had to return to Bony's palace.

"Give me a horse," cried King Bony, "for I shall have to capture them myself!"

Once more the prince and princess heard the sound of hoofbeats. "This time it is my father," said the princess, "but he cannot chase us beyond the first church in your father's kingdom. Give me your golden cross." The prince did so, and then the princess changed herself into a church, and him into a priest, and the horse into the church bell.

Up rode Bony. "Have you seen some travelers on horseback?" he asked.

"Just now Prince Unexpected rode this way with the princess, your daughter," said the priest. "They gave money for a mass for your good health and asked me to pay you their respects."

King Bony was forced to return to his palace empty-handed, for he could not travel beyond the church. Prince Unexpected and the princess rode on, and they had no more fear of being captured, so they rode gently. By and by, they came to a lovely town, and the prince was overcome by a great desire to go there.

"I have a feeling that misfortune will come of this," said the princess. "But if you must go, I will wait here in the shape of a white stone. The king and queen of the country will come to meet you, along with their daughter the princess, and a little boy. Whatever you do, do not kiss the little boy, for if you do, you will forget me at once, and I will die of despair."

Bony's daughter changed herself into a white stone upon the road. The prince rode into town, but he did not remember her warning. When the little boy rushed into his arms, he kissed the child. From that moment his memory was darkened, and he utterly forgot the princess, Bony's daughter, who lay as a white stone by the roadside one day, two days, three days. And when the prince did not return, she changed herself into a cornflower.

An old man came along the road and saw the beautiful flower. He dug it up carefully and carried it to his house, where he planted it in a pot, and tended and watered it. And from the moment the man brought the cornflower into his house, everything was kept clean and neat, and when he came home in the evening, dinner always awaited him. The man went to a wise woman to find out the reason for this wonder.

"You must get up before dawn," the woman advised him, "and notice what thing stirs first in the house. Whatever stirs first, cover it with this cloth, and you will see what you will see."

The old man didn't close his eyes the whole night. As soon as the first light of dawn appeared, he saw the cornflower leave the pot and begin to move about the room. The old man quickly placed the cloth on the flower, and the flower transformed into the princess.

"Why did you do this?" asked the princess, "I do not wish to live in this world. My promised husband, Prince Unexpected, has forgotten me."

"Prince Unexpected is to be married today," said the old man. "The wedding feast is ready, and the guests are beginning to arrive."

The princess wept, but then she dried her tears, and dressed herself like a simple village girl, and went to the palace kitchen, where she asked to be allowed to make the wedding cake.

The cake was served to Prince Unexpected on a silver dish. When he took a knife and cut into it, a marvel occurred. A pair of pigeons came out of the cake. The male pigeon walked away from its mate, who cried out,

> Stay, my pigeon, stay,
> Do not run away,
> Like cruel Prince Unexpected
> Who Bony's daughter did betray.

Prince Unexpected heard the pigeon's words, and all of a sudden, his memory returned to him. He rushed to the doorway, and behind the door he found Bony's daughter. He took her by the hand,

and they ran down the hall and out another door where his horse stood saddled and bridled. They rode until they arrived at the palace of Prince Unexpected's mother and father. The king and queen received them with joy and gladness, and before long they prepared a magnificent wedding, the like of which was never seen before or since.

The Magic Birch

[FINLAND]

 nce upon a time, there lived a man and a woman who had an only daughter. It happened that one of their sheep wandered off into the forest, and so the man and woman went searching for it, each in a different part of the wood. The good woman met a troll, who recited a magic charm, "Spit into my knife sheath, pass between my legs, turn into a black sheep." The woman became a sheep, and the troll took on the woman's face and form. "I've found the sheep," she called out to the good man. The man believed the troll was his wife, and never guessed that his real wife had been changed into the sheep. Home the two of them went, and when they got there the woman said, "We should kill this sheep, or else it will only run away to the woods again." The man, who was a quiet and peaceable fellow, made no objection, but only said, "Good, let us do so."

His daughter knew at once that the troll was not her real mother, and when she overheard this talk, she ran at once to the sheepfold crying, "Oh, dear mother, they are going to slaughter you."

"Well, then, if they do," replied the black sheep, "do not eat the meat or broth, but gather together all my bones and bury them by the edge of the field."

The troll made soup of the black sheep, and set it before the daughter, but the girl would not touch it. Late that evening, she carried the bones to the edge of the field and buried them, and from the bones a birch tree grew. Time passed, and a daughter was born to the troll. The two girls grew up together, but the troll's daughter was treated like a princess, while the older girl was tormented by her stepmother and stepsister.

Now it happened that a great festival was to be held at the palace, and the king invited all the people thereabouts, even the poorest and most wretched. And so in the good man's house, the troll and her daughter eagerly dressed in their finest clothes. The troll said, "Go along first, old man, and take our younger daughter with you. I will give the elder girl some work to do, so that she won't be bored while we are away."

When the two of them had gone, the troll threw a bowl of barley grains among the ashes in the hearth, and said, "If you have not picked every grain of barley out of the ashes, and put them back into the bowl by the time we return, I shall eat you up!" Then the troll hurried after her husband and daughter, while the poor girl stayed at home and wept. She tried very hard to pick up the grains of barley, but she soon knew that she would never finish by nightfall. So she dragged herself to the birch tree upon her mother's grave and cried because her mother was no longer there to help her. But in the midst of her tears, suddenly she heard her mother's voice saying, "Why are you weeping, little daughter?"

"The troll scattered barley on the hearth, and she has ordered me to pick every grain out of the ashes," said the girl. "That is why I am weeping, dear mother."

"Do not cry," said her mother. "Just break off a branch from the birch tree, strike the hearth with it crosswise, and the work will soon be done."

The girl took a branch and struck the hearth crosswise. In an instant, all of the barley grains flew into the bowl. Then she went back to the tree and laid the branch upon the grave. Her mother's voice told her to bathe on one side of the tree, dry herself on the other, then put on the clothes she found within the tree trunk. And when the girl had bathed, she became so lovely that no one on earth could rival her, and within the tree she found splendid clothing and priceless jewels, and a horse with hair partly of gold, partly of silver, and partly of something more precious still.

The girl rode swiftly to the palace. When she arrived, the king's son hurried out to meet her, and helped her dismount, and tied her horse to a post. He never left her side as she walked through the palace, and everyone stared, wondering who she was, but no one knew anything about her.

At the banquet the prince invited her to sit next to him in the place of honor. Meanwhile, the troll's daughter grabbed a piece of meat, crawled under the table, and was noisily gnawing the bones. The prince heard the sound and thought there was a dog under the table, so he gave a kick, and broke the arm of the troll's daughter.

Toward evening, the good woman's daughter thought it was time for her to depart, but as she left, all the people at the banquet ran after her. And so she took off her ring and threw it behind her. While everyone was looking for the ring, the girl mounted her horse and rode to the birch tree. She changed her clothes and tied up her horse there, and then she hurried to take her usual place in the ashes beside the fire.

The man and the troll arrived home a short time later, and the troll said, "You can't imagine what a fine time we've had at the palace. The prince liked my daughter so much that he danced with her and whirled her around. But look—the poor thing fell and broke her arm." The girl knew what had really happened, of course, but she smiled and said nothing.

The next day, they were again invited to the palace. "Hey, old man," said the troll. "Get dressed and take our child to the feast. I will give the other girl some work to help her pass the time."

When the father and daughter had gone, the troll threw a bowl of flax seeds among the ashes, and grinned, and said to the girl, "If you do not get all these seeds back into the bowl by the time we return, I shall eat you!"

The girl picked at the flax seed until she was sure that the troll was far away, and then she went to her mother's grave and took the birch branch, and struck the hearth crosswise with it, and all the flax seeds flew back into the bowl. Then she returned to the birch, and washed herself on one side of it, and dried herself on the other side. And in the tree trunk she found clothes and jewels even finer than before. A marvelous horse appeared for her, and she rode quickly to the palace, where the king's son came out to meet her, tied her horse to a post, and led her into the banquet hall. The girl sat next to him in the place of honor as she had done the day before. But the troll's daughter sat under the table gnawing on bones, and making a very disgusting noise. Again the prince thought he heard a dog that had no business being there, and gave a kick, and broke the troll child's leg.

When evening came, the girl hurried home again, this time throwing her golden circlet behind her in order to give herself a head start. She sprang onto her horse, and rode swiftly to her mother's grave, where she left her horse and her beautiful clothes. When her father came home from the feast with the troll, the girl was sitting in her usual place among the ashes.

Then the troll said to her, "You should have seen what happened at the palace! The king's son carried my daughter from one room to another— though he did let her fall, and broke her leg." The man's daughter smiled, but said nothing.

The next day, they were again invited to the palace. "Get up, old man! Take the little one to the banquet. I will give the other girl work to do while we are gone." This time she poured a bowl of milk on the ashes, saying, "Get all the milk back into the dish, and no ashes in it, or I will eat you up!"

The girl ran to the birch tree as soon as the stepmother was gone, and by its magic power the milk returned to the bowl, clean and white. Then she washed herself on one side of the tree, dried herself on another, and quickly dressed herself in a splendid gown and golden shoes, and rode off to the palace, where she found the prince waiting for her in the palace courtyard. He led her into the hall, where she was seated in the place of honor. But the troll's daughter crouched under the table, gnawing bones. Thinking it was a dog again, the prince gave a kick which knocked out her eye.

When evening came, the girl tried to leave the hall quietly, but everyone followed after her. So she had to throw one of her golden slippers to them in order to get a head start. Then she leaped onto the horse, and rode off, and when she reached the birch tree, she laid aside her fine clothes, and went into the house.

Her father soon came home with the troll, who began to mock her, saying, "Ah, you stupid beast! What wonderful things you missed at the palace. The prince carried my little girl about again—but she had the bad luck to fall and get her eye knocked out."

The girl ignored her, and went about cleaning the hearth.

The prince had kept the girl's ring, and her circlet, and her slipper, and now he made plans to find their owner. He called all the people of the kingdom to the palace for a fourth time.

The troll got her daughter ready. She tied a wooden washing bat in place of her foot, a pancake roller in place of her arm, and a piece of horse dung in place of her eye, and hurried her off to the castle. When all the folk were gathered, the king's son announced, "The maiden whose finger fits this ring, and whose head fits this circlet, and whose foot fits this slipper, shall be my bride."

The troll worked quickly to cut and file her daughter's head, and finger, and foot, until they fit perfectly. And so the prince was forced to take the horrid girl as his bride. Sad and confused, he accompanied her and her mother to their house. But when it came time for him to take his bride back to the palace, the girl who should have been his bride came forth from the ashes and whispered in the prince's ear, "Dear prince, do not marry the wrong sister."

The prince looked at her face and recognized her at once, and so he took both sisters with him. After they had gone a little way, they needed to cross a river. The prince threw the troll's daughter down, and she became a bridge, and there she remained for a long time, unable to move. "May a golden stalk grow from my navel, so that my own dear mother will recognize me," she said. And so it happened.

The prince took the cinder lass as his bride. Together they visited her mother's grave, where they received all sorts of treasures and riches— three sacks of gold and as much silver. They went to live in the palace, and in due time a baby boy was born to them.

Word of the child's birth reached the wicked troll, who believed, of course, that her own child was the baby's mother. She left at once for the palace, and on her way she came to the river. As she walked across the bridge, the troll noticed that a golden reed was growing there, and she decided to cut it and take it as a gift to her grandchild. As she did so, she heard a familiar voice say, "Please, Mother, do not cut me."

"Is that you, daughter?" asked the troll.

"Indeed, for the prince threw me here and made a bridge of me."

At once, the troll uttered a spell that shattered the bridge, and restored her daughter to her true shape. Then she ran to the palace, burst into the queen's bedroom, and recited this magic charm, "Spit into my knife sheath, bewitch my knife blade, become a reindeer."

The queen at once became a reindeer, and the troll used another spell to give her own awful daughter the beautiful face and form of the queen. But the baby prince knew she was not his real mother, and he cried so much that his father went to see a wise woman and asked what was making the baby so unhappy.

"Leave him here," said the wise woman. "I will carry him with me when I take my cows to the forest. Perhaps the trembling among the aspens will quiet the boy."

"Yes, take the child to the wood with you," said the prince.

So the woman took the baby to a place in the woods where a herd of reindeer grazed. Then she began to sing a magical song, and one of the reindeer came and nursed the child and cared for it all day long. The wise woman thought that this must be the child's real mother and she told the prince he should come to the woods with her the next day. The two of them built a fire by the edge of a marsh, and the prince hid. Then the reindeer came and began to nurse the child.

"Take off your reindeer skin," said the woman to the reindeer. "I will comb your hair for you." While the wise woman combed the queen's hair, the prince grabbed the reindeer skin and threw it into the fire. The baby's mother changed into a spinning wheel, then into a spindle, and she kept changing and changing into all sorts of things. But the prince smashed one after another, until at last his own wife stood before him again, and he embraced her, and took her home to the castle.

Then the prince ordered that a tub be filled with tar, and a fire lit under it, and the top covered with a blue cloth. He invited the troll and her daughter to bathe in the tub, and when they stepped on the cloth they fell into the hot tar and perished. But before they disappeared forever, the troll uttered a final curse, "May worms come upon the earth, and insects fill the air, for the torment of all humankind."

Tall, Broad, and Eyes-of-Flame

[CZECH REPUBLIC]

t all happened in the days when cats wore shoes, and when frogs croaked in grandmothers' chairs, and when donkeys clanked their spurs on the pavement like brave knights, and when hares chased dogs. So you see, it must have been a very, very long time ago.

In those days the king of a certain land had a daughter who was not only extremely beautiful but also remarkably clever. Many princes came from distant lands to seek her as their wife, but she would have nothing to do with any of them. At last she let it be known that she would only marry the man who could keep watch over her so well for three nights that she could not escape, and that those who failed would lose their heads. This news was announced through all the kingdoms of the world, and many kings and princes arrived and tried to keep watch over the princess, but not one was successful.

A certain young man named Matthias, who was prince of a royal city, decided to try for the hand of the princess. Matthias was agile as a deer and brave as a falcon, and he was eager for adventure. But his father did not want him to go and risk his life. In fact, he forbade his son to do so, but nothing he said could dissuade the prince. What could the poor father do? At last, worn out with arguing, he gave Matthias his blessing, filled his purse with gold, and watched as his son went off to seek his fortune.

As he traveled, Matthias met a stout man who was walking along rather slowly.

"Where are you going?" Matthias asked him.

"I am traveling all over the world in search of happiness."

"What is your profession?"

"I have no profession. But I can do something that no one else can do. I am called Broad because I can puff myself up to such an immense size that there is room for an entire regiment of soldiers inside me." He held his breath and swelled up until his body blocked the road.

"Bravo!" shouted Matthias. "Would you like to accompany me? I, too, am traveling across the wide world in search of happiness."

"If there is nothing bad in it, I am certainly willing," answered Broad, and they continued their journey together. A little further on they met a man who was nearly as tall as a house and thin as a pin.

"Where are you going, my good man?" asked Matthias, who was extremely curious about this stranger's appearance.

"I am traveling about the world."

"To what profession do you belong?"

"To no profession, but I am called Tall, and with good reason. Without leaving the earth I can stretch up and touch the sky. When I walk I clear a mile at each step." Without more ado, Tall stretched himself until his head was lost in the clouds.

"What a fine fellow you are!" Matthias shouted up to him. "Wouldn't you like to travel with us?"

"Why not?" answered Tall.

So the three of them went on their way together. While passing through a forest they saw a man who was busy piling huge tree trunks one upon another.

"Who are you, my good man, and what are you doing with those trees?" asked Matthias.

"I am known as Eyes-of-Flame," said the man, "and I am about to make a fire." So saying, he stared at the wood until the whole pile burst into flame. "I can also see for a hundred miles in all directions," he added.

"You are truly a powerful chap," said Matthias. "It would please me mightily if you would join us in our travels."

"All right, I will," answered Eyes-of-Flame.

So the four of them travelled along together. Matthias was delighted to have three such talented companions, and he shared his money with them, never even complaining about the huge amounts of food that Broad ate. Matthias told them the purpose of his journey, and promised to reward each one handsomely if he succeeded in winning the princess. In return, they gave him their word that they would use all of their powers to help him. Matthias bought them fine clothes, and when they were all presentable, he sent them to tell the king that a young man had come with his attendants to watch three nights in the princess' chamber.

The king received them very politely. "Think carefully before you begin this task," he told them, "for if the princess succeeds in escaping, you will all have to die."

"We cannot imagine that she will be able to escape from us," they replied, "but come what may, we intend to try. Let us begin at once."

"It was my duty to warn you," replied the king, "but since you insist, I will lead you to my daughter's dwelling."

Matthias was dazzled by the loveliness of the royal princess. She received them all graciously, admiring also the prince's good looks and gentle manner. Night was approaching, and so Broad sat down and stretched himself across the doorway. Tall and Eyes-of-Flame stood near the window, and Matthias sat near the princess, watching her every move lest she escape.

Suddenly the princess said, "I feel as if a shower of poppies were falling on my eyelids," and she lay down on the couch, and seemed to fall asleep. Matthias did not breathe a word. He tried to watch the princess, but then he, too, began to feel drowsy. His eyes closed, and so did those of Tall, Broad and Eyes-of-Flame.

This was the moment the princess had been waiting for. Quickly she changed herself into a dove and flew toward the window. But the tip of one of her wings touched Tall's hair. He awakened, and called to the others. Eyes-of-Flame watched the dove as it flew, and his gaze burned the ends of its wing feathers so that it could no longer fly. The dove was forced to alight on the branches of a tree. Tall hurried to the tree, stretched up, caught the bird, and placed it in Matthias' hands, where it changed back into the princess.

The next morning, as well as the morning after that, the king was quite surprised to find his daughter still sitting by the stranger's side. He said nothing, but entertained the four men royally. However, when the third night approached, he spoke with his daughter in private and begged her to use all her magic powers in order to escape these strangers, for no one knew what kind of men they were or where they came from.

Matthias took his comrades aside that evening and said, "Just one more night, dear friends, and we shall succeed in our quest. But do not forget that if we fail, our four heads will roll."

"Never fear," replied the three. "We will keep good watch tonight."

When they came into the princess' room, they went to their usual places. Broad sat in the doorway, Tall and Eyes-of-Flame stood by the window, and Matthias sat facing the princess, trying not to let his eyes close. By midnight, though, sleep was beginning to overpower the watchers. The princess stretched out on the couch and shut her eyes as if she were asleep. Matthias admired her in silence, but as sleep closes even the eyes of the eagle, so it shut those of the prince and his companions.

The princess, who had been watching them all this time through nearly-closed eyes, soon changed herself into a fly, and escaped through the window. As she flew above the palace well, she changed again into a fish, and dropped down into the dark water. She surely would have escaped, except that when she was a fly she had touched the tip of the nose of Eyes-of-Flame, causing him to sneeze. He opened his eyes just in time to see the fly change into a fish and fall into the well. He called out to his companions, and all four of them ran outside. The well was exceedingly deep, but that did not matter, because Tall soon stretched himself so that his feet could reach the bottom. He searched in every corner and crack of the well, but still he was not able to find the fish.

"Get out now, and let me try," said Broad, and he let himself down into the well. Then he puffed himself out until all the water rushed up into the air. But still no one saw the fish.

"Now it is my turn," said Eyes-of-Flame. As soon as Broad had climbed out of the well, and the water had returned, he set to work. As he gazed at the water, it began to grow hot. It bubbled and boiled, and then the companions saw a little fish throw itself up onto the grass and change into the form of the princess.

"You have won the contest," she told Matthias. "Now I am your bride both by right of conquest, and by my own free will."

The young prince's courtesy, strength, and gentleness may have pleased the princess, but her father was not ready to accept a stranger as his son-in-law, and he announced that he opposed the marriage. Matthias and the princess had no choice but to run away, along with Tall, Broad and Eyes-of-Flame.

The king was furious, and ordered his guards to follow them and bring them back, alive or dead. It was the princess who first heard the sound of their pursuers, and she asked Eyes-of-Flame to look and see who was behind them. He told them that he saw a great army on horseback that would soon overtake them.

"They are my father's guards, and they will be difficult for us to escape," the princess said. She took the veil from her face and threw it behind her saying, "I command as many trees to spring up as there are threads in this veil."

In the twinkling of an eye, a high thick forest grew behind them, and the soldiers had to stop and cut a path through it. Matthias and the princess were able to get far ahead of them, and even had time to stop for a rest.

"Look and see if they are still coming after us," said the princess. Eyes-of-Flame looked back and reported that the guards were out of the forest and advancing towards them at top speed. So the princess let fall a tear from her eye and said, "Tear, become a river." Then a wide river appeared between them and the guards, and it took the army a long time to get across.

"Eyes-of-Flame," said the princess after a bit, "is anyone following us now?"

"They are quite near to us again," said Eyes-of-Flame. "In fact, they are almost on our heels."

"Let darkness cover them," said the princess. At this command, Tall stretched until he reached the clouds, and his head half covered the face of the sun, casting darkness upon the advancing army. But Matthias and his party, whose path was lit by the other side of the sun, were able to travel swiftly onward. Finally, Tall uncovered the sun and joined his companions, taking a mile at each step. The palace of Matthias' father was in sight when suddenly they noticed that the royal guards were again close behind.

"Now it is my turn," said Broad. "Go on your way in safety while I remain here." Broad quietly awaited the horsemen's arrival, standing still as a statue, his chin upon the road and his mouth open from ear to ear. The royal army charged forward, mistaking Broad's mouth for one of the city gates. They rushed inside, and disappeared. Broad closed his mouth, then ran to rejoin his comrades in the palace of Matthias' father. His stomach was a bit upset, what with a whole army inside, and the earth groaned and trembled under his feet as he ran. He could hear the shouts of all the people assembled around Matthias as they rejoiced at his safe return.

"Ah, here you are at last, brother Broad," cried Matthias. "But where is the army?"

"The army is quite safe," answered Broad, patting his enormous person. "But I shall be happy to be rid of them, for the horses are particularly difficult to digest."

"Come then, let them out of their prison," Matthias urged.

Broad stood in the palace square, put his hands to his sides, and began to cough. And at each cough, horses and horsemen tumbled out of his mouth, one after another. The last one had a difficult time getting out, for he had lost his way inside one of Broad's nostrils, and was unable to move. It was only by giving a good sneeze that Broad could get him out. Once they had been released from Broad's stomach, the soldiers lost no time in returning to their own kingdom.

A few days later a splendid feast was given at the wedding of the prince and princess. Tall had been sent to invite the princess' father, and owing to the length of his legs, he arrived there before the royal army. The king was delighted to know that his daughter was to be married to a rich and noble prince, and Tall persuaded him not to punish his soldiers. Matthias rewarded Broad, Tall, and Eyes-of-Flame generously for their service, and they remained with him to the end of their days.

About the Tales

No one knows for certain how old fairy tales are. A tale from an Egyptian papyrus dated 1250 B.C. contains many magical elements found in fairy tales. The oldest story with a complete fairy tale plot is "Cupid and Psyche" by the Roman writer Apuleius. Much of medieval literature resembles fairy tales, but unfortunately, these texts contain very little information about the oral tradition which was clearly their source. Studies of nineteenth and twentieth century European stories and storytellers, along with historical evidence, strongly suggest that fairy tales have been passed on by word of mouth since before the invention of writing.

The telling of long fictional stories has now nearly vanished with the advent of mass media, and fairy tales today exist almost solely in books and on film. But modern media does not allow tales to change and adapt as they once did, when master storytellers fine-tuned their tales to please and enlighten their listeners. Even so, fairy tales still exert a strong power over the imagination. They have a richness of metaphor and symbol that is the result of centuries of collective shaping and reshaping, and people continue to be drawn to them as resources for contemplating meaning.

Fairy tales have been recorded almost exclusively in Europe, in surrounding regions, and in areas settled by Europeans. In the nineteenth century, after thousands of oral tales had been recorded, researchers found that the number of basic fairy tale plots was limited, and at the same time, there seemed to be countless local variations. Antti Aarne and Stith Thompson categorized fairy tale plots into a few hundred "tale types." Differing versions of one tale type were called "variants." Variants of a single tale type from one culture resemble each other, but individual storytellers were free to change and adapt tales to some extent. Narrating a fairy tale was never a matter of word-for-word recitation, but rather of retelling a familiar story in a way that was at once traditional and individual, and always to please a particular audience.

No fairy tale should be interpreted or analyzed by looking at a single version. For example, several interpretations of "Red Riding Hood" have focused on the color of the heroine's cap in Charles Perrault's tale. French folklorist Paul Delarue compared hundreds of oral versions collected in all parts of France in the nineteenth and twentieth centuries, more than one hundred years after Perrault's fairy tales were first published. He found that in oral tales, the color of the girl's cap or hood was nearly always either white, yellow or green, and seldom red. A search for meaning might better focus on the fact that the heroine of these tales wears a cap or a hood, rather than on its color. Another interesting difference between Perrault's and the oral versions of "Red Riding Hood" is that traditional storytellers had the heroine use her wits to escape the wolf, while Perrault chose to portray her as a victim. A knowledge of variants allows us to distinguish between significant and insignificant details, and between traditional tale elements and ones that may have been invented by a single person, or that might even have resulted from mistakes in transcription or translation.

The relationship of fairies to fairy tales is a mystery to many modern readers. To understand European fairy beliefs, one must discard the literary image of fairies as tiny, cute winged creatures. In folk beliefs recorded across Europe, supernatural beings closely resembling humans were said to inhabit a parallel otherworld. Though the names of these beings varied from region to region, beliefs about them were remarkably similar. Fairies could be helpful or harmful to humans. They might point out buried treasures or bestow healing skills, for example, but they were also known to kidnap people, and lead them astray. In Celtic areas of Europe, a person who died young was said to have been "taken" by fairies, who cleverly left a corpse resembling that person in their place. Legends tell of ways a "taken" relative could be brought back from the fairies' realm. The otherworld abode of the fairies was said to lie underground, or inside a mountain, or underwater, or across a body of water. Even today, the burial mounds and stone structures of Neolithic peoples are said to be the dwelling places of fairies. The content of fairy tales is closely linked to folk beliefs recorded in rural areas of Europe well into the twentieth century.

Folktale collectors remarked that fairy tales were often told with seriousness and respect that could best be described as religious. Wilhelm and Jacob Grimm first proposed the idea that fairy tales had their origins in pre-Christian religion. This idea has long been out of favor, but it deserves serious consideration, especially given fairy tales' close resemblance to Greek, Norse, Slavic, and other early European mythologies. It seems likely that fairy tales originated in one or both of the two major early cultures of Europe, Neolithic and Indo-European. Fairy tales about heroes who ride magic horses and abduct princesses express an Indo-European warrior ideology, while tales in which princesses choose their own husbands and use magic to win them are closer to goddess myths of old Europe. Both cultures spanned much of the European continent. That stories very much like fairy tales were a vital part of these cultures would help explain the wide diffusion of similar fairy tale plots. The tale notes that follow are based on this assumption, and so I sometimes explain part of a fairy tale from one region using folk beliefs, legends and rituals recorded in another area.

The following notes identify the print sources of the fairy tales in this book. (Unfortunately, most early editors did not identify the tales' tellers.) Tale type numbers are given, and these can be used to find variants, with the aid of Aarne and Thompson's *Types of the Folktale* and Ashliman's *Guide to Folktales in the English Language*.

In the notes, I give examples of how each tale relates to the oral storytelling tradition and to other aspects of folk culture. These notes are necessarily far from complete, due to space limitations, and because many features of these tales remain a mystery to me. The books in the bibliography on page 186 are all highly recommended for further reading. I have edited the tales, some a little, others a lot. Many of the source texts were translated into a dry, academic English. In my retellings I attempt to provide an oral narrative style that reads well aloud, without altering the tales' content.

1. The Three Princes, the Three Dragons, and the Old Woman with the Iron Nose (Hungary). W. Henry Jones and Lewis L. Kropf, *Folk-Tales of the Magyars* (London: The Folk-Lore Society, 1889). Translated from János Erdélyi, *Népdalok és Mondák* (1846). Tale type 300A, *The Dragon-Slayer. The Fight on the Bridge.*

Slavic fairy tale heroes often possess horses that speak, foretell the future, and fly. They acquire their horses in various ways. Some must outwit and trap their magical steeds. Hatching such a horse from an egg is a traditional motif. Many-headed animals are common in fairy tales, though the Tátos (from a Hungarian word meaning shaman), with its three heads and five legs, is unusual. The dragon of Slavic fairy tales seems to shift between serpent and human shape as the plot requires.

This dragon was identified with storms, and was said to ride a horse, accompanied by a wolf and a raven.

The otherworld was sometimes described as lying across water—on the other side of the river Styx in Greek myth, or across the sea in Celtic myth, for example. It could be reached by boat, by flying, or by magic bridge. In this tale, the bridges are made of the triad of metals often associated with the otherworld: gold, silver and copper. The Norse goddess Freya, like the old woman in this tale, was depicted riding in a cart drawn by two cats. When Ambrose descends under the earth, the tale's plot shifts from the *Dragonslayer* type to a version of *The Search for the Lost Husband* recounted from a male point of view. Usually this latter tale type is told from the point of view of the heroine, as in "The Three Daughters of King O'Hara" and "The King of the Crows" in this collection. The motif of a villain's life force lying outside the body is common in fairy tales, though the heart is nearly always said to lie in an egg.

2. Fair Angiola (Italy). Thomas Frederick Crane, *Italian Popular Tales* (Boston: Houghton, Mifflin, 1885). Translated from Laura Gonzenbach, *Sicilianische Märchen* (1870). Tale type 310, *The Maiden in the Tower*.

"Fair Angiola" resembles "Rapunzel" in the Grimms' collection, but the plots of the two tales diverge after the heroine meets the prince. Imprisoning an unmarried maiden in a tower is a common fairy tale motif (see "Ivan Goroh and Vasilisa Golden Tress" in this collection). These attempts are always unsuccessful.

Many fairy tale heroines are said to be six or seven years old when they encounter a female character such as a witch or evil stepmother. In peasant societies, this is the age at which a girl begins to work for her family, tending animals and learning household skills. During this transition, a mother or other female relative who had formerly been loving and undemanding might indeed seem to be an evil witch. In many fairy tales, witches are somewhat mean and somewhat loving. They are also sources of knowledge, power and gifts. It was from the witch, no doubt, that Angiola learned the magic she used in her escape. The folktale motif of a chase, in which objects thrown on the ground grow and block pursuit, is found worldwide. Another method fairy tale heroines use to avoid capture is shape-shifting, as in "Prince Unexpected."

3. The Wild Man (Sweden). Benjamin Thorpe, *Yule-Tide Stories* (London: Henry G. Bohn, 1853). Translated from Gunnar Olof Hyltén-Cavallius and George Stephens, *Svenska Folk-Sagor* (1844). Tale types 502, *The Wild Man*, and 530, *The Princess on the Glass Mountain*.

In some tales of this type, a wild man helps a couple conceive a child, then returns to claim the baby. In variants from Brittany, the wild man is named Murlu or Merlin. After the young hero of a wild man tale goes out into the world, there is no one standard plot line. The wild man may help the hero defeat a dragon, or give him a magic horse to use on a quest.

Some Slavic folk beliefs situate the entrance to the realm of the dead atop an iron or glass mountain. In Lithuania, amulets containing bear or lynx claws were often worn, and were buried with the dead, even in this century. The purpose of these was to help the deceased ascend the mountain. Golden apples have a range of positive magical associations, including youth, eternal life, and marriage. A golden apple was a passport to paradise in both Greek and Celtic myth. In fairy tales, the golden apple is often the object of a quest, along with the water of life and the magical bird.

4. Tatterhood (Norway). George Webbe Dasent, *Popular Tales from the Norse* (Edinburgh, Scotland: Edmonson and Douglas, 1859). Translated from Peter Christen Asbjørnsen and Jørgen Moe, *Norske Folk-Eventyr* (1852). Tale type 711, *The Beautiful and the Ugly Twin.*

Variants of this tale type have been collected almost exclusively in Norway and Iceland. Male and female roles are usually quite conventional in fairy tales. Tatterhood is one of the few fairy tale heroines who rides into battle or sails a ship to foreign shores. The tale contains interesting suggestions of older religion. Gods of the Celtic otherworld were pictured riding on goats, as was the Greek goddess, Aphrodite. The Norse god Thor rode in a carriage drawn by goats. In many Scandinavian folktales, goats are the enemies of trolls.

The wearing of a hood was associated with otherworld beings in Norse folk belief and mythology. A tattered hood may signify the placenta, or caul, which was widely believed to have magical powers. Wooden ladles were used in women's birth rituals in Latvia and Lithuania in the nineteenth century; wooden ladles in the form of ducks have been found at Neolithic sites in these same areas.

5. The Thirteenth Son of the King of Erin (Ireland). Jeremiah Curtin, *Myths and Folk-Lore of Ireland* (Boston: Little, Brown, 1890). Tale type 300, *The Dragon-Slayer.*

The behavior of birds is widely believed to have significance for human affairs, as in the beginning of this tale. Sean Ruadh is one of many Irish cow-herding lads who rescues a damsel from a monster. There may be a kinship between this type of fairy tale hero and the mythological American cowboy.

Notice how allergic Sean is to commitment. Three giants and a serpent frighten him less than claiming the princess as his bride. In most dragonslayer tales, another man boasts that he killed the dragon, and the real dragonslayer then must fight this human foe to claim his reward. Identification of a reticent hero by means of a shoe, Cinderella style, seems to be uniquely Irish. Celtic fairy tale dragons usually arise from the sea, rather than descending from the sky like their Slavic counterparts.

6. King Lindorm (Sweden). Andrew Lang, *Pink Fairy Book* (London: Longman's, Green, 1897). Translated from Eva Wigstrom, *Folkdiktning* (1881). Tale type 433B, *King Lindorm.*

Many fairy tales begin with an unwise or careless action by a man or woman which has terrible consequences for their unborn child. When parents resort to magic or make hasty, poorly-worded wishes for children, offspring who are part animal are often the result. These children usually require the help of a mate in order to achieve human form, though the method of disenchantment varies from gentle to violent, even among variants of the same tale type told in the same area. This tale element may have been at the discretion of the individual storyteller.

In the source text, this tale contains a further episode in which the bride's stepmother continues to persecute her after marriage. It is very confused, and I chose not to include it.

7. Ivan Goroh and Vasilisa Golden Tress (Russia). Jeremiah Curtin. *Myths and Folk-Tales of the Russians, Western Slavs, and the Magyars* (Boston: Little, Brown, 1890). Translated from Aleksandr Afanas'ev, *Narodnye russkie skázki* (1855-64). Tale type 300, *The Dragon-Slayer.*

The motif of conceiving a child by swallowing a pea or a bean or other small object is found in myths and folktales throughout the world. Few fairy tale heroes are ordinary. Many are backward, lazy or unpromising—at least in their parents' opinion. Some, like Ivan Goroh, are supernaturally gifted from the start. Ivan behaves more like a hero of myth or epic than of fairy tale, and has been likened to the Slavic thunder god, Perun. In many variants of this tale, it is the princes' mother, not their sister, who is abducted by the dragon. The character of Baba Yaga is often helpful to Russian fairy tale heroes, reserving crueler treatment for heroines. Still, Ivan is careful to show her the respect that he himself has learned from fairy tales.

8. The Three Daughters of King O'Hara (Ireland).
Jeremiah Curtin, *Myths and Folk-Lore of Ireland* (Boston: Little, Brown, 1890). Tale type 425, *The Search for the Lost Husband*.

Tir na n-Og, the land of youth, is an Irish name for the otherworld. In variants of this tale, the animal shape of the lost husband may be a bear, bull, wolf, snake, hog, hedgehog, frog, bird, or tree, reflecting the belief that the souls of the dead may enter into animals and plants. This tale seems at its deepest or oldest level to be about bringing someone back from the land of the dead. Death also enters into this tale in the form of the crow that carries off the three babies. The damage done to the little girl by her mother's tear provides a concrete example of the folk belief that too much grief can harm a departed loved one in the afterlife. This tale type's connection to death beliefs probably escapes most modern readers. The fact this tale type is still read and appreciated (a Norwegian variant, "East of the Sun, West of the Moon" is frequently reprinted) demonstrates the adaptability of fairy tale symbols and metaphors.

9. Three Golden Hairs of Grandfather Allknow (Czech Republic). Karel Jaromir Erben, *South Slavonic Folk-Lore Stories* (London: Forder, 1899). Translated from Erben's *Slovanská čítanka* (1865). Tale type 461, *Three Hairs from the Devil's Beard.*

Three Fates are known from ancient Greek tradition, and appear in the works of Homer and Hesiod. The thread of life was said to be spun by Clotho, measured by Lachesis, and cut by Atropos. Similar goddess triads are known from other traditions, for instance, the Laima in Baltic countries, the Germanic Norns, the three Brigits in Ireland and the Roman Parcae. The fairies who attended the christening of Sleeping Beauty are seven in Perrault's tale, and thirteen in the Grimms' "Briar Rose," yet Wilhelm Grimm found that in nearly all oral versions there were three gift-giving fairies. The Fates embody the belief that a person's life is determined at or before birth. Their gifts to Floatling describe the life of the typical fairy tale hero: he will come into great dangers, escape all dangers, and marry a princess.

The punishment of the king in this tale is especially neat. Like the tsar in "The Firebird and the Horse of Power," Floatling's father-in-law seals his own fate by trying to imitate the hero. He is thus justly punished without any of the other tale characters getting their hands bloody. The harshness of a villain's punishment in fairy tales varies so widely that it seems to have been at the discretion of each storyteller—guided by the tastes of their listeners, of course. In the nineteenth century, most storytellers were members of the lower classes, and were known to be especially hard on upper-class fairy tale villains who abused their authority.

10. Twelve Wild Ducks (Norway). George Webbe Dasent, *Popular Tales from the Norse* (Edinburgh, Scotland: Edmonson and Douglas, 1859). Translated from Peter Christen Asbjørnsen and Jørgen Moe, *Norske Folk-Eventyr* (1852). Tale type 451, *The Maiden who Seeks her Brothers.*

The wish for a girl child in this and other fairy tales arises from the old custom of inheritance by the youngest daughter. She was expected to perform all the rituals necessary to assure her parents' and siblings' well-being in the afterlife. Spinning thistledown would be an impossible task for a mortal, though fairies could easily do it. Many fairy tales include an after-marriage episode in which the heroine's mother-in-law or stepmother accuses her of murdering her own children. Such episodes are frequently found in oral Cinderella tales.

11. How Ian Direach Got the Blue Falcon (Scotland). John Campbell, *Popular Tales of the West Highlands* (London: Alexander Gardner, 1893). Tale type 550, *Search for the Golden Bird.*

It doesn't seem to matter how or why the hero or heroine of a fairy tale leaves home, at least insofar as the plot is concerned. It only matters that they do, and in Celtic tales, this is often accomplished by one character placing a magical obligation on another. Whether the motivation of the person who sends the hero on a quest is good or bad, the result is always good for the hero. The helpful, shape-shifting fox or cat is a standard fairy tale character, in variants of *Search for the Golden Bird* and also 545B, *Puss in Boots,* for example

Ian Direach engages freely in trickery and theft, which is common in fairy tales. Such behavior tends to be censored or rationalized in printed versions. For instance, "Jack and the Beanstalk" has been rewritten to justify Jack's thefts from the giant on the grounds that the giant had originally stolen the magic objects from Jack's father. It is important to realize that in fairy tales, tricks and theft have a symbolic and mythical dimension. The hero or heroine brings treasures back from the otherworld into this world, just as Prometheus stole fire from the gods for the good of humankind.

12. The King of the Crows (France). Jean-François Bladé, *Contes populaires de la Gascogne* (Paris: Maisonneuve and Larose, 1885). Translated by Judy Sierra. Tale type 425, *The Search for the Lost Husband.*

The collector-editor identified five storytellers as his sources for this tale, and he also recalled hearing the tale as a child from his grandmother. Like many editors, Bladé combined several different oral tellings into one printed text. Though only one teller described the Green Man as having a single eye, Bladé chose to include this detail in his composite. Anyone reading a group of variants of the same tale type from the same region will understand why editors create composite texts. Each individual telling has its strengths and weaknesses. A blend of tellings is often necessary in order to fashion a rich and satisfying tale—or sometimes just a readable tale. This is not really a travesty of tradition, because a person in a storytelling community would hear the same tale many times from more than one storyteller.

The description of the wedding of the Green Man's daughter makes it quite obvious that the "crow" is a dead man, in this case a powerful king. In beliefs recorded in the west of England, the soul of King Arthur has been said to inhabit the body of a raven or chough. Similar beliefs about the souls of dead kings in the form of birds were reported in ancient Greece. In Celtic countries, encounters with female fairies often took place at wells and springs. Reported sightings of fairies in these locations may have been due to people's imagining they saw human shapes in the mist and fog that hover above bodies of water. Washing was a task fairies performed especially well, in addition to spinning and weaving.

13. The Enchanted Toad (Sweden). Benjamin Thorpe, *Yule-Tide Stories* (London: Henry G. Bohn, 1853). Translated from Gunnar Olof Hyltén-Cavallius and George Stephens, *Svenska Folk-Sagor* (1844). Tale type 402, *The Mouse (Cat, Frog, etc.) as Bride.*

It is unusual for a fairy tale hero to accomplish his quest in quite so passive a manner as this one. The tasks set for him by the toad may seem odd, but they are related to rituals that have survived into the twentieth century in rural parts of Europe. Ceremonial structures made of trees and branches, such as the English maypole, were decorated with bits of ribbon, cloth, colored paper, etc. These structures were associated with different festival days in different countries (May Day in England, Midsummer Day in Sweden) and were sometimes left standing until midwinter, when they were burned. This hero's performance of simple, repetitious tasks is probably related to the patience and self-discipline required of those who carry on religious traditions. The image of the toad and her entire court being disenchanted simultaneously is reminiscent of the Grimms' "Briar Rose." "The Enchanted Toad" could be a telling of a Sleeping Beauty tale from a male perspective. Folklore collectors noted that male and female storytellers told the same tale types differently.

14. Oh, the Tsar of the Forest (Ukraine). R. Nisbet Bain, *Cossack Fairy Tales and Folk-Tales* (New York: Frederick A. Stokes, 1895). Bain cited Ukrainian folklore collectors Panteleimon Kulish, Ivan Rudchenko and Mykhailo Drahovaniv as sources for the tales in this collection. Tale type 325, *The Magician and his Pupil.*

In *The Interpretation of Fairy Tales,* Bengt Holbek theorized that the supernatural villains in fairy tales were none other than the familiar characters of rural life. To a farmer or other manual laborer, any master of a skilled trade might indeed have seemed like an evil magician. For example, millers were often portrayed as diabolical characters in folktales because they earned a good living without working very hard. In a Russian variant of this tale, a helpful father seeks a master for his son who will teach him the skills which enable some people to "eat much, dress well, and work little." Shape-shifting competitions between a master and a pupil are common in fairy tales.

15. The Firebird and the Horse of Power (Russia). Arthur Ransome, *Old Peter's Russian Tales* (London: Thomas Nelson and Sons, 1916). Translated from Aleksandr Afanas'ev, *Narodnye russkie skázki* (1855-64). Tale type 550, *Search for the Golden Bird.*

In Slavic tales and legends, the firebird was said to feed on the golden apples of youth and to have a song that healed the sick and restored sight to the blind. One of its feathers could illuminate the darkest room. In many variants of this tale type, the hero is a simpleton and/or a mistreated youngest son who succeeds because of his kind actions toward animals, who later help him in his quest. The search for the firebird leads to marriage for the hero. In a heroine tale from Russia, a princess falls in love with the portrait of a prince and secretly commandeers her magician-father's firebird and rides it to the bedchamber of the prince.

16. Prince Unexpected (Poland). Albert Henry Wratislaw, *Sixty Folk-Tales from Exclusively Slavonic Sources.* (London: Elliot Stock, 1889). Translated from Antoni Josef Glinski, *Bajarz polskí* (1862). Tale type 313A, *The Girl as Helper in the Hero's Flight. Youth Promised to Devil.*

Like many fairy tale heroes, Prince Unexpected receives magical assistance from his enemy's daughter and later marries her. The tasks Bony assigns the prince are ones which, according to folk belief, only fairies could accomplish. Master builders were rumored to have gotten their skills from otherworld spirits, for example. Fairies could confuse the senses of mortals, making them see whatever they wished them to see. Identifying one's fairy sweetheart from among her lookalike sisters was a common "impossible task" in fairy tales and legends. Fairy folk were also believed to be exceptionally speedy shoe-makers. According to a German legend, an elf once made a pair of shoes for a shepherd during the time it took him to stir his porridge.

This tale ends with a forgotten fiancée episode. When a fairy tale hero forgets who his true bride should be, and plans to marry another, she reminds him in one of two ways. She may produce a pair of talking birds, as in this tale, or she may ask him a riddle, typically, "I have a lock, and I lost the old key and got a new one. Now I have found the old key. Which key should I keep?" By either method, she manages to return him to his senses. This type of episode occurs frequently in tales in which the heroine helps her fiancée escape from the otherworld ruler.

17. The Magic Birch (Finland). Andrew Lang, *Red Fairy Book* (London: Longmans, Green, 1890). Translated from Eero Salmelainen, *Suomen kansan satnja ja tarinoita* (1857). Tale types 510A, *Cinderella*, and 403C, *Witch Secretly Substitutes her own Daughter for the Bride.*

This is not the only variant of tale type 510 that begins with the murder of the good mother; in some variants from Greece, her elder daughters kill her. A central image of oral Cinderella tale is the gift-giving tree that grows on the grave of the real mother. Like many fairy tale heroines, this one must undergo further attacks after marriage. The scene in which the queen goes through a series of transformations is similar to widely-recorded (and supposedly true) accounts of how a stolen spouse or lover has been rescued from the fairies.

18. Tall, Broad, and Eyes-of-Flame (Czech Republic). Karel Jaromir Erben, *South Slavonic Folk-Lore Stories* (London: Forder, 1899). Translated from Erben's *Slovanská cítanka* (1865). Tale types 513, *The Extraordinary Companions* and 313, *The Girl as Helper in the Hero's Flight.*

A princess who orders her suitors killed appears in many fairy tales. The heads of her victims may even sit atop the fence posts around her castle. Her bloodthirsty ways don't seem to make her any less appealing as a potential bride! This motif has been interpreted as expressing symbolically the intense emotional impact of rejection upon a young man. Helpers with unique, often supernatural powers who assist the hero or heroine on a quest are found in folktales worldwide. These companions may be animals, people, or even personified objects. They serve as a memory aid for the storyteller: their abilities, which are easy to visualize and recall, determine both the kinds of problems the hero will encounter and how the helpers will solve them.

Selected Bibliography

Aarne, Antti, and Stith Thompson. *The Types of the Folktale.*
Folklore Fellows Communications no.184. Helsinki:
Academia Scientiarum Fennica, 1961.

Ashliman, D.L. *A Guide to Folktales in the English Language.*
Westport, Conn.: Greenwood Press, 1987.

Fraser, James. *The Golden Bough.* New York: Macmillan, 1922.

Gose, Elliott. *The World of the Irish Wonder Tale.* Toronto:
University of Toronto Press, 1985.

Graves, Robert. *The Greek Myths.* New York: Penguin, 1960.

Grimm, Jacob. *Teutonic Mythology.* New York: Dover, 1966.

Holbek, Bengt. *The Interpretation of Fairy Tales.* Folklore
Fellows Communications no. 239. Helsinki: Academia
Scientiarum Fennica, 1987.

Kamenetsky, Christa. *The Brothers Grimm and Their Critics.*
Athens: Ohio University Press, 1992.

Kravchenko, Maria. *The World of the Russian Fairy Tale.*
Berne, Switz.: Peter Lang, 1987.

Lüthi, Max. *The Fairytale as Art Form and Portrait of Man.*
Bloomington: Indiana University Press, 1984.

Propp, Vladimir. *The Morphology of the Folktale.* Austin:
University of Texas Press, 1986.

Sierra, Judy. *Cinderella.* Phoenix, Ariz.: Oryx Press, 1992.

379